LAZARUS

A NOVELLA

CHRIS KAUZLARICH

PHANTOM QUILL
PRESS

For Graysen and Justin.
My fireflies in the dark.

CHAPTER ONE

Kami didn't see them coming until it was almost too late, the crunching of glass in the dark alleyway being her only warning. Her heart raced, the blood pumping at quickening intervals choreographed to the rhythm of her legs. She had almost won first place when she was still on the track team in school before the Recession hit... before the street. Now she did little more than scurry after rats in the gutter just for a spot of protein, at least, that was until tonight.

She smacked a rusted trash can over that was sitting next to the dumpster, feeling a pang of relief with the even louder crash and outburst of curses that followed.

"Catch that bitch!"

How many of them were there?

Tires squealed off to her right, instinct telling her to go toward the noise instead of away from it. The car flew past her as she turned the corner onto the main road, and a new screech tore into the night; the puddles on the street glowed red as their brake lights erupted onto the scene.

"Shit," she hissed.

Her pace quickened, and she felt the strain of unused muscles resisting her call, malnutrition and complacency taking their toll. She didn't know how long she could keep up the pace, only knowing that stopping would likely be her end. Rumors had been spreading that other kids on the street had been vanishing, never ones that came from families of consequence, mind you, just those society forgot about. Everyone had forgotten about Kami when her father shot himself, losing his job along with three hundred others at the plant, even her Mama, who just couldn't cope. Kami had come home from school one day, and Mama was gone, the house locked up tight. From that point on, she was a vagrant, and the neighbors made sure the police were called, believing at their core that their family never belonged there.

The street turned dark very suddenly, and the disorientation from her pupils attempting to adjust made her misstep, twisting her ankle and falling to the pavement. She clenched her teeth as she tried to rise on her hands, blood trickling from the fist-sized scrape on her cheek.

All the streetlights were out, the realization causing a cold sweat to flourish between her shoulder blades.

Kami fought the urge to scream, her breathing flowing out of her in whooping huffs on the verge of hyperventilation. This was how the other children were captured... there was coordination. New York City never slept, yet the street was clear; somehow, they could control her artificial sense of comfort: the lights.

"Mama—"

Her whispered cry cut off as she put her weight on her ankle before collapsing again with a gasp. There was no way to move forward, the pain being too great. A car slowed to a stop beside her as she pulled herself across the sidewalk, the sound of the window rolling down and her wheezing the only thing her ears registered.

"Can't help but feel for the little street rat; she's still trying. This is a good one." He admired her; the inflection was plain to anyone listening, her very existence sounding as commodified as a stout pair of reliable shoes.

"Just fucking do it already. We only have a two-minute window on these lights."

A cat peered at her from under a newspaper stand a few feet away, watching as a thunk noise— like a ball launched from a tube— preempted a pinch in her shoulder. Her muscles seized, and she fell forward, numbness washing over her body. Kami tried to open her mouth but to no avail, and as she lost focus on the world around her, the cat came into view a final time, a rodent securely in its jaws.

Nothing like losing a game of cat and mouse.

CHAPTER TWO

"Ladies and Gentlemen! Thank you so much for attending this little party!"

The crowd laughed, passing glances at one another and taking in the entire ballroom around them. This little party was actually quite a large shareholder celebration, six hundred strong. Lazarus, Inc. had a record-breaking sixteen months since they secured United States Food and Drug Administration compliance, and they intended to bask in their fortunes with every decadence available. Corks popped as servers carrying white cloths, dressed in black, moved with surgical efficiency between guests like SS officers at a rally in Munich circa 1936, offering glasses of Armand de Brignac Brut Gold Champagne with an accompanying napkin of beluga caviar and foie gras. Glasses clinked, and the shuffling of bodies and chairs put a pulse on the event, a building hum of energy and anticipation.

Jarum Daughtry watched from his dais on stage, taking it all in, feeding off it—a parasite draining its host. All of this was due to his vision. The grandeur, the pomp, and, oh, the profits. He learned the mistakes of the other biotech firms, watching them take one fatal move after another, all with the same goal: preserving youth and eliminating disease.

Thasia Labs was the first to die, their immortality failing despite what the origins of its name implied. Koschei GmbH was the next to go, followed closely by YWS. The human genome was a tricky mistress, and all of them had the key to the vault, something a little corporate espionage revealed and helped to further his own endeavor, but they did their execution all wrong. Eradicating Alzheimer's and heart disease were admirable goals, even his ailment for that matter, but when in America had anyone truly thrown money at a cause solely focused on good intentions?

Where was the manipulation of the consumer? The invoking of the deep seeded need for American consumerism? It needed pizazz and sex appeal. Fountain of Youth? Lazarus had the answer. Like the proverbial biblical figure, Jarum's company had the means to resurrect, in a manner of speaking, for a price. Debilitating diseases could be pushed aside, delivering hope via a short infusion and the great ol' American dollar. The infirm would have the clock turned back for the rest of their lives, and Jarum Daughtry was the savior.

Kenny Hotchkins, Lazarus's COO, clinked his glass with a Montblanc pen and waited as the noise quieted to continue. The subtle sound of fabric shifting against chairs carried in the air like the whisper of flapping wings as he held his gaze on the crowd just as sharply as Jarum. He could feel the goosebumps cascading along his arms as he felt a near-orgasmic thrill at their captivation. The cameras were rolling, and he smiled, teeth gleaming, his mouth becoming the pearly white gates with the answer to the eternal question.

"Today, we saw something nobody ever thought possible. For years, researchers have looked for that next step—that missing piece that will complete the puzzle of disease and aging among our fellow man. Trial and error, decades of contentious ethical debates, studies, failed endeavors, and religious stonewalling seemed to create an impenetrable barrier to success. But no more."

Kenny paused, turning around to lock eyes with Jarum, preparing him for his declaration. Inhaling deeply and sweeping his gaze across the room for maximum effect, Jarum stepped forward, pulling the room into his vortex, the sheer force of his presence.

"Ladies and Gentlemen, I give you our CEO, Jarum Daughtry."

An eruption sounded throughout the banquet hall as the two men shook hands, and Kenny stepped aside. Kenny had always been a loyal friend, and at times even more, but the one thing Jarum could rely on, above all else, was his idolatry, with Jarum being the golden calf.

"Kenny Hotchkins, everyone," Jarum said, clapping as his accomplice waved to the crowd of shareholders.

"I couldn't ask for a better COO. With his help, what he has alluded to couldn't have been possible, but it is. Today, I am pleased to announce that we officially have certification for our treatment, the only one of its kind to go mainstream for the public. Lazarus Inc. holds the keys. No longer must we watch our elderly suffer the debilitating effects of dementia, our children suffer from incurable congenital disabilities, or, more deplorably, see the results of bad plastic surgery on our celebrities." A boom of laughter filled the room as Jarum scrunched his nose as if catching a whiff of something distasteful. They were captivated. They were his.

A hush descended—signaled by his upraised hands—preceding his gaze taking the room in, one quadrant at a time, filling every attendee with the sensation that Jarum was looking directly into their eyes, speaking to them.

"My friends. My colleagues. My fellow visionaries. Tonight is our night. Drink, eat, and celebrate. Tomorrow... we take the world."

The applause was thunderous, rippling through formal attire in shades of noire, an impending storm warning of its imminent deluge. Ripples formed as Jarum stepped off the dais, the sycophants closing in, reaching out to touch the cloak of the most high, hoping for a brush with greatness, the man who shaped the fortunes of those in the room from mere millionaires to billionaires. Their eyes were glazed, their admiration a trance.

Jarum was pleased.

CHAPTER THREE

Whrite light. It was everywhere. The rhythmic blip of something mechanical carried on the air intertwined with a whiff of something sterile like bleach, completing the olfactory tango; the physicians dance. More beeping, different than the blip, but on its own interval. Hours passed, or so it seemed to, the exact amount of time known only to those who were free. Kami wasn't so lucky.

Every so often, she tried to turn her face, but she couldn't. Was she numb or restrained? She couldn't tell; her body no longer felt like her own. Where was she? Her throat moved, straddling the line between involuntary and forced, a dull ache of the unused muscles radiating outward, focusing her attention elsewhere. Had she been able to swallow this whole time? She tried it again, and the ache was no better, but the result seemed slightly improved. Kami did this several more times, each time trying to rein in the drool she now felt trickling down her cheek, a torment amounting to self-induced water torture.

With each passing moment, she regained consciousness and control over her motor functions and sense of self. Flashes of that last night on the street started returning to her, the raspy sound of the man speaking of her as if she was his next purchase. He had called her a street rat.

"Fucker," she mouthed, no actual sound escaping her cracked lips. Christ, it hurt.

The white light receded, zooming out as awareness crept in, her sight freed from the perception of a telephoto lens. Strips of halogen bulbs streaked across the ceiling above, no longer an indistinct blob of incandescence, revealing unblemished ceiling tiles, and just off to her left, a silver hook with a half-filled bag tethered to it. The contents were yellowish, and something about the sight of it made her stomach drop. She inhaled sharply, and her heart began to race. As her panic overtook all notion of calm and rationality, she felt her chest palpitating, and a burst of sweat bloomed along her arms and neck, soaking through the thin sheet covering her skin. Rasps of air, in and out, tried to force their way into her already congested spectrum of hearing, the thrumming of her blood, in tune with her heart, pulsing like the overwhelming bass of the crescendo, stealing the show.

Red, like looking at the sun with your eyes shut, closed in around her, a corona circling the white, losing focus. Whispers. Voices drawing closer.

"...panicking... going to need Sublimaze... low dose... save plasma..."

Kami felt a pinch, but it was far off. Or did she? Everything was a haze, like being lost in the mist, directionless. Suddenly a breath. A sharp inhalation, cold and clean. Her eyes shot open, and her body tensed. She was wet, drenched, actually. Did someone pour water on her? Her body jumped, that slight quiver of the unexpected, as two people in doctor's smocks and masks looked at her, one of them moving a bright light back and forth across her face, causing afterimages of light that oscillated with every blink.

"You still with us?" The doctor on the right's mask moved, so Kami locked her eyes on hers, trying to plead through her intensity of gaze.

"She understands, alright," said the other on the left, and they both stood up straighter, looking off at something above her head. Kami took another deep breath, not realizing she'd been holding it. Their stares frightened her, especially the one on the left. He had malicious eyes, and his voice carried the same weight.

"Heart rate at 147. She's dropping. Let's give her a few more minutes to stabilize."

"What difference does it make-"

"Come on, B. She's a kid."

"And that's your problem. You need to stop looking at them as more than what they are."

The doctor on the right sighed loudly, looking down at her a final time. She had kind eyes, green flecked with brown, like Kami's Mama.

Beep, beep, beeeeeeppppp

"Let's go. We're being paged. Another empty."

"We're really cooking now, huh," mean-eyes said excitedly as he left Kami's field of vision.

"Yeah, it's great."

Lingering a moment longer, kind eyes met her gaze, an unspoken transmission of remorse, and then she walked away. Kami was left alone again. It was just her, the rhythmic beeps, and the memory of her Mama's eyes.

CHAPTER FOUR

Ruth had suffered for so long, whole days merging with others, life evaporating. Miracle cures were never really something she bought into. Growing up, it was much more common to pray to Jesus, and everything would turn out alright, but too often in her life, these pleas for aid went unheeded. A husband that was there for his children, for starters. Some things never changed. She doesn't recall what dementia was, she just knew she had it, and her daughter found a place that could help with that. Life would be simpler if she were just left to float away like the white seeds of a dandelion once their vibrancy expired, but humans were a stubborn lot, and her daughter was as bad as they came, adamant she pushed on. Why couldn't she understand how tired Ruth was?

She stared at her shoes, not remembering how to Velcro them, the tiny flaps needing a horizontal assist, mere inches from their destination. She sighed.

"Mom, are you ready?"

Julia was always an impatient child, too quick to boss people around and never observing the human condition.

The passage of time and motherhood only amplified her demeanor.

"Mom. What the hell? I have to pick Stacie up in two hours! Will you—never mind." Julia knelt and pushed the black Velcro strap down, securing Ruth's shoes.

"That's it!" Ruth felt triumphant as the memory returned, and a quick flash of doing the same for Julia when she was a girl occupied her mind. Those bright blue eyes met hers, black pigtails bouncing excitedly at her new shoes she could do herself.

"Julia?" The words came out slowly. Shakily.

The young girl dissolved around those eyes into something hard and lined with the wear of middle age. Julia sighed; a whiff of coffee breath and patchouli perfume danced within reach of Ruth's nose.

"I hope this works. Let's go."

Ruth got to her feet, pins and needles pirouetting up her thighs as she straightened. She must have sat in place for too long. When had time become such a force that worked against her?

"Julia dear, you should cover up."

Ruth moved her shaky finger and wagged it in line with her daughter's chest. Her shirt hung low, revealing more than Ruth would have dared to even in her heyday, granted times were different. Women walked around with skin-tight pants, like panty-hose, with obscene things written on their rear ends. Ruth didn't waste her time with Jesus anymore, but she would send thanks his way that her daughter and granddaughter had more discretion. Her eyes landed on her daughter's half-exposed breasts once more.

Most of the time.

Julia gave Ruth's finger a small swat, and the expression on Julia's face said everything. Ruth lowered her gaze and started walking, slowly at first but picking up steam like a locomotive, knowing her daughter had had enough. Anything to get her away from that look on her daughter's face. What would happen to her when she finally lost her faculties? What would Julia do to her?

The air was crisp yet fresh. Flashes of fireflies and apple pie nudged at the back of her consciousness, memories of a time thought forgotten yet piercing through to the present, confusing her. The fireflies continued to swirl, fluttering at the edges as little pinpricks of light trying to take center stage.

She gave her head a slight shake, the curls of her bouffant bouncing ever so delicately.

"We're close, Mom. You feeling alright?"

"Hmm, what—um, yes, fine, dear."

Julia squinted at her mother, scrunching her eyebrows. Her condition seemed to worsen, and lapsing out of the present for long periods became more frequent. Again, she hoped this would work.

She looked forward again and turned onto Fifth Avenue. Julia knew her mother thought she was a bitch. On more than one occasion during a lapse, Ruth even told her exactly what she thought of her. Cold, heartless, and vile were only a few of the descriptors used. She hadn't wanted to be this way, or at least to be thought of as such; it was just who she was. This is how she cared. She was efficient, and interruptions didn't get the things done that needed to be accomplished.

The light turned red, and Julia stopped the car, briefly looking at her mother. Ruth looked so small, helpless even, but Julia knew the fire beneath that buildup of amyloids in her mother's brain.

"Your husband left you because you're an icy cunt!" That stung to think about.

An elderly couple stood at the stoplight waiting to cross, arm-in-arm, the embodiment of companionship. What kind of life did they have? Which one of them would slide toward the abyss first? Did it matter as long as that person was there, unwavering in devotion?

A horn blared behind Julia, and she gave a start.

"Whoa, okay, buddy. Jesus! I'm getting as spacey as you, Mom."

Ruth didn't acknowledge her daughter as the car moved forward again. Her words had drifted somewhere at the periphery, just heard but no more significant than a bird chirping in the park. The main focus was the buildings and the people. How had she gotten there? She could have sworn that she was on her porch just minutes before, with cinnamon wafting and floating jewels of light flashing in the valley, a deep buzzing drowning out all sound. Yet, that seemed wrong, didn't it? Ruth hadn't been in a valley, and she knew that for truth, just as much as she knew that from where she sat, she could no longer see the sky or the clouds. It was stifling.

"Julia."

"Yes?"

"Could you roll down the windows? It's ever so stuffy. It had been crisp...."

"Um, right. Ok. Well, we are just about to pull up to the Medique, so we'll be getting out."

"Right." She sighed, feeling defeated.

Julia stopped the car in front of an elegant-looking building, a French chateau amidst the modern lines of the other New York City shops. A woman approached, all labels, little C's turned in opposing directions printed on half her wardrobe. There was a look of weathered elegance about her, a young person with just a bit of fraying along the unseen edges.

The valet drove off as Ruth and Julia entered, and her breath caught as she took in the scope of the interior, the outer facade paling in comparison to its grandeur. Crystals sparkled overhead from the prominent chandelier, acting as the focal point above the display cases aligned like those at a fancy jeweler, the French kind. Blonde women dressed in all-black pantsuits carrying tablets greeted them before accompanying them to one of the display cases.

"Welcome to Lazarus Medique. Do you have an appointment?"

Her skin was perfect, with no trace of a wrinkle or blemish, even with her broad smile showing too many teeth. Something was off with her eyes, though. Ruth felt it.

"Yes, we do. 12:20 for Ruth Jarlsen."

Julia sounded intimidated, almost meek. The up-speak at the end of her sentence startled Ruth. Why did she sound like she was asking?

The woman's smile broadened as her fingers maneuvered over her tablet with expert efficiency, never looking up yet captivating them nonetheless.

"Ah, yes, here she is. Ruth, so nice to meet you."

Her voice had taken on a husky, haughty quality, and all Ruth could think of was that blood girl from a decade ago who tried to act like the founder of that Apple company. All the women here had that same disturbing demeanor, those piercing, artificial stares.

A pattern of C's caught Ruth's eye, and she realized the woman from outside was talking animatedly to another of the blondes, staring hungrily at the display cases. Ruth looked down, noticing the actual product for the first time.

They were glass vials, crystal even, filled with a rich amber liquid, spaced out to maximize simplicity, and featuring a name printed on heavy card stock in front of each one. It was mesmerizing.

"Ruth?"

"Hmm. Yes?"

"Excuse my mother. That's why we are here." Julia was biting her lower lip, forehead wrinkled. Ruth realized she must have wandered again.

"Absolutely. Are you Julia? Julia Rankin?"

"Yes, that's right."

"Ok, it says here that you have power of attorney, so I can direct my questions at you."

Julia nodded. She looked pale.

"Have you chosen the product you'd like for your mother? Our success rate is extraordinary, but some vintages work better than others. I suggest something a bit more robust for your mother. May I?"

The blonde woman swept her arm out over the display case like a magician vanishing a card. Those eyes didn't change.

"I suggest the Ambrosh31. It's an exquisite vintage. The donor was extremely hardy. We want to make sure we are achieving maximum results. This is more than cosmetic."

She lifted the bottle out of the case and placed it on a velvet pad, her hands shielding it if unwelcome hands attempted to touch it. The woman watched Ruth and Julia, appraising them.

Ruth turned to look at her daughter over her shoulder and saw her unconsciously running a finger along a wrinkle on her cheek. Julia started, dropped her hand, and straightened her posture. That was more of what Ruth expected to see from her.

"Why exactly do we need something of this... potency?" Her hands moved in a wafting motion as she debated which word to use, and one of the security guards near the door turned toward them, sweeping his jacket back to reveal his holster; a warning.

The blonde made a subtle motion with her hand, dismissing him when she realized Ruth was following.

"My apologies. We get a lot of protestors in here. Any animation by a guest is watched for our safety. Can you believe it? People tell us we need to stop playing God," her shoulders bounced subtly along with her throaty laugh; it was deep and artificial.

A buzz echoed from that laugh, like millions of tiny wings.

Ruth frowned and grabbed Julia's hand. She shook her mother off and looked at the security guard wide-eyed.

"Honestly, no worries, Mrs. Rankin—"

"Ms. Rankin," Julia interrupted. It was brusque with a hint of vulnerability.

"My apologies. Ms. Rankin. Let's get back to the topic at hand. We suggest such a high vintage because of the youth of the donation, tied with the vitality of the donor. We have seen a direct correlation between those factors and overcoming cognitive decline. This is a far more pinpointed approach than using any old blend."

"Right... that makes sense. Let's go with that one. Is the cost higher?"

"$80,000."

"Wha- $80,000. Will my insurance cover any of that?"

"Technically, it's your mother's insurance, and since we have FDA certification as of a few days ago, we've been circled in for Medicare approval. It's no longer billed like cosmetic surgery and can be coded the same as other medical treatments."

Julia breathed, and her shoulders relaxed, settling back down.

"I have a question."

They both turned to Ruth, and the force of their scrutiny made her want to shrink into the floor, to become invisible, like a cell.

"Um, well... what do I have to do?"

The blonde's smile returned and she swiped up the bottle of liquid amber.

"Why it's a simple transfusion. Your appointment was set for treatment today, so we will take you to the back and get you set up. We will have you in and out in no time, Mrs. Jarlse-"

"Just Ruth. My first name is fine if you are sticking me with a needle."

She leaned her head back and let out the husky, robotic laugh again—the fireflies signaling just in her periphery.

"Ruth it is."

Passing through a door like a bank vault, Ruth was unnerved by the changes in her surroundings from the showroom. Everything was white, and the prominent smell of isopropyl alcohol and the bright LED spotlights overhead disoriented her. She grabbed Julia's arm for stability as they passed room after room like it was a hospital hidden from view by opulence. Ruth smiled. *Look over here, something shiny.*

They entered a room to their left that housed a dentist's chair and a machine resembling a water cooler without the heavy jug. A small black mechanical arm extended off to the side of the device, a long thin needle sticking straight out from it.

The blonde opened the top of the machine and poured the amber liquid inside; blue indicator lights sprung to life around the upper rim and began emitting a subtle pumping noise.

"What exactly is that liquid you plan on giving me?"

The woman straightened, eyes empty and face looking more unnatural than ever before.

"Why Ruth, I thought you knew. It's plasma, and an extraordinary kind at that. You are about to receive the Elixir of Life."

The buzzing erupted to a steady hum, drowning out everything, as fireflies engulfed her, feeding the void.

CHAPTER FIVE

oneysuckle flowed on the breeze, coming in waves like perfume spritzes tickling her nose. The pollen was heavy this time of year, and the beauty of the rolling hills of lush green grass and wildflowers had its price; a vista this perfect wouldn't be free. Kami resumed her walk, sniffling as she looked out toward the horizon. She knew she shouldn't have spent the day rolling around the hills and looking for rocks to collect, but how often would she get the opportunity in the desert of concrete that was New York? Geology was one of her favorite classes in school, something neither of her parents understood, but it fits with her solitary nature; just as running did. Her mind was always somewhere all alone, and she wanted to keep it that way.

A pinch caused Kami to flinch as she crested the hill that looked down on the wooden cabin. The pain started subtly but grew in intensity with each step. The world began to spin a little faster, and her breathing became more shallow, the cabin moving farther away the closer she should have come to it. An odd buzzing reverberated in her ears, and a bee floated past her, flying from the scene of its crime.

"What the hell did I do to you?" she called after it. The sting looked mean and red, throbbing worse than any bruise. The buzzing got louder, and the bee began changing, appearing like a giant stinger without its body.

Dust billowed as she collapsed to the ground, tremors starting in one appendage and traveling to the next, like an electrical current conducting on the sweat excreting from her every pore.

"Mama!"

Her cry was desperate yet restrained, not due to her lack of trying. Kami's throat didn't want her voice to escape, instead allowing only unintelligible grunts to enter the silence. She tried again and again, every time being no more successful than the attempt before it.

A familiar breeze passed over her once more, carrying the scent of the honeysuckle paired with a new fragrance, lavender. Whispers of shuffling grass traveled in its wake, and a pair of eyes filled the blue void of the sky before her, stray fireflies lighting up like a halo behind them. Both were green, flecked with brown; savior's eyes. A hand caressed Kami's forehead, unseen but easily identified, and through that touch, she felt the need to sleep. She made one last attempt to speak and was able to muster just enough for a single word as the safety of the cabin floated away like a dandelion seed on the wind.

"Mama."

Blip, blip, blip. The incessant noise droned on, matching the rhythm of her heart and the throbbing in her arm. Kami felt empty, sucked dry as if every ounce of her life force had evaporated. What was happening to her?

Once, when she still ran cross country in school, Kami forced herself ahead into a sprint, moving faster than she ever had, until her legs gave way. The drop in her heart rate was a shock to her system that had brought on extreme lightheadedness and nausea, but she had won, spilling over the finish line mere inches ahead of her competition. It was a fatigue that stayed with her the rest of that day and didn't even compare to what she felt now.

Kami inhaled, and it felt like something was compressing her chest. The effort was extraordinary for just that single breath, and she didn't think she could take another. How had something her body had done on auto-pilot become like this? She strained to suck in another deep breath—like inhaling through a straw—and began coughing, sending needles through her chest. Thick mucus came up her throat, and she spat it out, forcing her eyes open.

Like so many times before, white light filled her entire range, a visual companion she couldn't seem to shake. Her breathing was labored, she could finally hear it over the *blips,* and she wondered how long it would be until the end. What an odd thought. Could it already be the end? Was this the great mystery, death being just eternal pain?

Lavender with a hint of honeysuckle pierced through the haze and sharpened her focus. Something eclipsed the bright white, and a face started to materialize into some-thing recognizable amongst its muted glow; green flecked with brown, the most beautiful sight she'd ever seen.

"Mama."

It came out as a hoarse croak but had finally been audible. The eyes lowered, a crease developed along her brow, the bottom half of her face covered. This wasn't Mama, Kami realized. The exposed skin was a milky white, not the amaretto of her mother's. This was the doctor who hesitated—the one with the kind eyes.

Moisture ran down Kami's face, and she realized she was shedding tears yet had no physical or emotional attachment to them. It was as if she sprung a leak she had no control over, but it was the defense mechanism she needed. Kind-eyes wiped beneath Kami's with a gloved hand and gently rubbed her cheek.

"I can't do this anymore...."

It came out as a murmur that Kami knew she wasn't meant to hear. *Then don't,* she had wanted to say but held her tongue.

Kind-eyes sighed and pulled her hand back, conveying compassion she had not seen since before Mama vanished. Kami still couldn't reconcile why she had gone... or had she? Maybe like Kami, she had been taken. She'd held it against her mother these last few months, but deep down, she couldn't believe that her Mama had truly abandoned her.

Beep, beep, beeeeeeppppp

Kind-eyes looked over her shoulder and froze. The indecision was plain. What horrors must the woman have seen or conducted? She swept a loose piece of hair from her face and turned back to Kami.

"It will all be over soon. I am sorry you had to go through this. They had said-" she cleared her throat. "They had said this," she lifted her hands, sweeping them in the air, "was for the benefit of everyone, to heal the sick. How was I-"

Beep, beep, beeeeeeppppp

She froze again and looked over her shoulder.

Kami followed her gaze to the camera in the corner and felt her tension.

"I'm sorry…" she whispered.

Something stirred in Kami, Mama's wisdom perhaps. Anytime Kami had questioned something she knew the answer to, her mother would give her the 'wisdom.'

Now, Kami, you know what happens to us. You should have thought this through, Mama had told her, not unkindly, the time she had to pick Kami up from the police station. She had been brought in for shoplifting, something Mama had lectured about at length. Kami tried to explain that she wasn't responsible; her 'friends' had stolen those sweaters while she was in the fitting room, but her Mama wouldn't have it.

No excuse.

Those girls knew what would happen if Kami was with them, and they had invited her for a reason. They were light-haired and light-skinned, and Kami wasn't. She knew better, those girls having an edge that made their opinion of authority quite clear, and yet, she went anyway, learning Mama's wisdom the hard way. So much for a generation that was color-blind.

From then on out, any time something felt off, and she asked her mother about it, she would get a level stare and *"remember your 'friends'"* as a response. Kind-eyes needed to remember her *'friends.'*

"Then help…" It came out as a guttural sound, startling the woman. Her hand extended before pulling back as if burned, then again more slowly before hovering just above Kami's hand; she lowered it without touching her.

"I want to," she paused, crestfallen. "I can't. I shouldn't even be talking to you. I'm sorry."

A squeal peeled through the silence as she turned away

from Kami on her heel, the noise transporting her to another place.

Boys ran back and forth playing basketball on the court, their side-to-side scrimmage a symphony of rubber and physics. She came every day after school to watch and listen, stimulating her senses. Shawn would always escort her home when practice was over. It would be quiet then, Old Spice drifting to her nose as she held his arm, his skin always warm from the exertion and post-game shower. He had been her first kiss. Nothing fancy or romantic, just a minute or two in the alley before her house. It was wet but perfect, at least to her. He was the first boy she remembered going missing. Less than a week after, her father shot himself.

"No." It was no more audible than her last attempt, but the sound of her hand banging the bar gave the emphasis that was needed. Mama was in her, and she'd had enough.

"You are—" Kami inhaled deeply," responsible for this... You knew the company—" a wheeze and cough before pressing on, "you kept. You will help."

Another slam of her hand punctuated her demand. The woman turned, watching Kami struggle to get the words out. Her eyes remained kind but were wide, her hands fidgety. Kind-eyes looked like she had seen a ghost while also being laced with the nervous energy of a rabbit eyeing a fox, tensed for flight.

Kami wanted to say more, feeling like she needed to lock down the woman while she held her attention, but all her energy had just been used. She was empty. Silence stretched between them, emphasizing the beeping of the medical machines like crickets on a warm summer night in the country. They held each others' gaze, and with another *'beep, beep, beeeeeeppppppp'* kind-eyes fled.

"No... please," Kami heard herself say, but the flash of blue was gone, followed by the metallic slam of a heavy door.

"Coward." Her voice was hollow, and she lay there, motionless. Despondent. Hope had finally been in front of her, she could taste its sweetest, and just as quickly, it became a fleeting thing, gone as fast as the glimpse of a shooting star. All that remained was darkness and pain. Her eyes closed and drifted off into the void.

CHAPTER SIX

Jarum took a deep breath, looking at his reflection in the mirror. He'd finally made it; he'd done what he set out to do. His skin was smooth, and his color was rosy and full of life, so different from the diagnosis that ate away at him when he started this process.

"Are you almost done in there," Kenny called, and Jarum exited to the bedroom.

Kenny lay in the bed, the mussed sheets only covering his midriff and his hair damp with sweat. They grew up together, went to college together, and formed this company together, and throughout that time had been more, on and off, but it gave Jarum what little he needed for release.

"Care to rejoin me?" Kenny asked, patting the bed.

"Too much to do. Our little interlude was enough."

Kenny lowered his head and stood up.

"Maybe later," Jarum said. His voice didn't hint at trying to mollify Kenny's feelings, but he tried his best to take it that way.

Jarum twitched, swerving his head to the left. Kenny watched him, following his gaze. Nothing was there.

"What is it?"

"Nothing," Jarum said, and Kenny furrowed his brow with concern.

"The car is being pulled around. I'll meet you downstairs."

Kenny nodded and saw the expression on Jarum's face change; something behind his eyes flipped, like a breaker, activating something else, this hardness that'd been growing of late. Jarum had always been borderline ruthless, not with Kenny but to others, but this change behind his eyes... could it be like the reports that came in, the mental break of a few past patients?

Kenny shook his head as Jarum left the room, banishing the thoughts. Jarum was fine.

"So what are the current results?" Jarum asked as he sat at the head of the boardroom table, Kenny taking the seat at his right.

"We've had promising results that align with what we shared with the FDA. The latest round of plasma infusions has shown near-perfect success in curing a terminal ailment in a patient. That was out of the recent sample of 1,363 recipients."

Martha Cohn, Chief Product Officer, was on the edge of her seat as she recited the data, her excitement hardly contained.

"Near perfect?" Jarum asked, raising an eyebrow. If there was one thing he couldn't tolerate, it was imperfection, not with something as crucial as Lazarus, not with something that involved his own salvation.

Martha flushed, sliding back into her seat.

"One recipient had an allergic reaction to the transfusion that caused anaphylactic shock; another had a heart attack immediately after, likely due to the inelasticity of their veins and the surge of fluid to their heart. They both died. A third still lives but had a psychotic episode about two weeks after the treatment. Their dementia is gone, and time's seemed to reverse the aging of their skin, but mentally...."

"That's a small margin, though, considering our sample size," Kenny said, trying to lighten the mood. "We should be happy with this."

Martha jumped on Kenny's enthusiasm.

"Yes, we should! Look, our success rate is currently 99.76%. Who has ever had a rate that high?"

"What of the synthetic replication we've kept promising? That has not been successful, Martha."

All eyes shifted to Rodney Thomas, Chief Legal Counsel. Jarum's eyes bore into him, and Rodney was one of the only people who didn't flinch from them.

"We don't speak of that," said Jarum icily.

"This is the only place we can, Jarum. The FDA will catch up to us eventually on this. I don't know how you've kept loyalty thus far, but it will be found out, let alone think of the ethical implications. We can't do what we've been doing forever. People may have let it slide when we used inmates, but children-"

"Rodney, enough!" Jarum stood, fists slamming on the table.

"All the people we've helped justify what we've done. Every single one of you: Martha's melanoma, Kenny's father's Hepatitis, Connor's wife's stroke, Sidney's heart disease, your ALS, and my-" Jarum stopped to catch his breath and lowered his head.

He looked up again slowly, his eyes meeting Rodney's.

"We've all been brought together by tragedy. For all the good we've done, Rodney. Synthetics? We'll get there, but for now, the sacrifice is necessary. The inmates were too old. Their plasma was just as riddled with decay from natural mutation as those it was supposed to help. You all know this. The children... for each of them sacrificed it has saved hundreds if not thousands."

Jarum's voice was slow and determined, but something menacing lurked beneath. They'd all seen what he was capable of, what he demanded for the sake of the greater good. Kenny knew Jarum thought he was doing the right thing no matter what happened, but he also relished the profits. He isn't sure when it changed, but outside of the moral question, Jarum would kill for what he'd achieved: his conquering of death and wealth.

"We won't stop until we've eradicated disease. Period. I'll be willing to sacrifice thousands more donors to save millions. Which one of you wouldn't?"

Jarum's voice was ice, his eyes as hard as an executioner's.

"Look, Rodney, these children had nobody, just like the inmates. I don't see how you are justifying that latter over the former anyway," Kenny said, trying to diffuse the tension. "We've done so much good. The charities, the decreased rate of disease, all of it is due to us. Will you bring this up to Lurie's or St. Jude's? Are you going to be the one to tell those parents that the treatment they've been promised for their children is being taken away?"

Rodney's defiance was broken, withering away under Jarum's gaze and Kenny's verbal onslaught.

"Anyone else? I'm right here," Jarum said, arms wide, a fighter preparing for his match.

"The mental health spike with our patients?" Sidney asked meekly, trying her best not to poke the bear but always trying to keep the facts front and center.

"An outlier," Jarum said dismissively. "We've identified the specific genetic markers causing the issue and have a possible solution. It will take time, but those outliers fall into our margin of 0.24%, correct?"

Everyone around the table nodded.

"Codename Bethany," Kenny said quietly.

"Bethany," Jarum agreed.

"Until that time, we need to continue our media blitz and show the true strengths of our treatments. Some of our more recent plasma distillates have led to extraordinary changes. Every iteration has led to further advances in not only reversing a disease but overall cosmetic health as well. The recent change of that woman in New York, for example. I want her for interviews, and we must see how to preserve her donor. That combination is gold."

"The sheer amount of blood needed to generate enough plasma makes it impossible to," Sidney started but stopped short, cut off by Jarum's gaze.

"Any means necessary. I'll see you all tomorrow," Jarum concluded.

His word was final.

CHAPTER SEVEN

T he room was cold, her breath puffing as steam when she entered. These rooms were always as crisp as a Spring morning, but they plummeted as soon as a "donor's" vitals flatlined, the sensors and failsafes kicking into gear to preserve the product and prevent rot. The alerts for disposal had been frequent, accelerating as demand increased after the FDA issued approval. It was exhausting.

A shiver ran through her. The eyes staring up at her were open, lifeless, the mouth ajar ever so slightly. She felt nothing. She knew she still had the ability, crying herself to sleep and waking most nights screaming from night terrors in a cold sweat; images of the lifeless eyes watching her. Bennet told her more than once to push the thoughts away, but she wasn't as forbidding as him. She couldn't simply push something like that out. The pressure was starting to get to her, especially after Am31.

She knew better than to make eye contact; it was part of the demeanor modification training put in place as the program grew, and fear of a conscientious objector plagued the thoughts of the CEO. Too many early "elixir" start-ups were brought down by whistle-blowers, mortified by unethical medical studies and advancements. She'd allowed herself to ignore so much for the greater good... but the nightmares haunted her.

They began as mere flashes, waking her with a sense of unease, always around 3:00 AM, the weak pleas for help and the lifeless eyes.... Over time, they progressively worsened as the pressure came down the chain of command, urging her team to start clinical trials and take everything from the donors. But at what cost?

When the first donor died, everyone on the medical floor was in a state of shock. Would this mean the end of the company? A German competitor had recently been shut down for a death; certainly, American agencies would be just as strict, if not stricter, wouldn't they?

The first couple of days passed in tension, a held breath waiting to be exhaled, and then unexpectedly, another donor expired from the sheer volume of blood extraction. Certainly, they'd have to cease operation.

The CEO released an internal memo celebrating the beginning of the FDA's standard review and championing the organization's pioneering spirit. He never once addressed the dead donors or, as she finally allowed herself to acknowledge, the children.

So many kids... and yet another in front of her. The small yellowish hand rested on the bedside rail, so still, it was almost beautiful, like a still-life. Everything was inert, calm, not even a breeze. The silence made her ears hunger for the chorus of her emergency room clinicals, the telemetry beeping and the *ding ding* signaling an intravenous infusion completing its course. All the sounds of God-fearing mortality trying to cheat its hand, with her as the dealer. No longer, as evidenced by the gentle hum of the cooling system and the subtle buzz of the LEDs overhead, her new symphony as she became the undertaker.

"It's about damn time, Violet."

She flinched, never sensing Bennet walk into the room, lost in an auditory vacuum of thoughts.

"Jesus B, you scared me."

"Obviously. What took you so long? The fucking system beeped, I don't know how many times."

"Yeah, sorry. I was caught up."

"Am31?"

Violet's face flushed.

"What? No. I mean, she was on my rounds earlier, but I was only in there for a few minutes."

Bennet stared at her, his eyes blank and mean. He was there the first time she let herself get caught up by Am31. Those eyes entreating for help... *Mama,* she had called her. Violet squeezed her eyes shut to clear her mind of the girl's voice, her pleas. She couldn't be seen as weak or sympathetic, especially in front of Bennet. He wouldn't hesitate to report her.

Bennet turned to look at the camera in the corner and gave his head a nod toward it. Violet sucked in her breath. Had he seen?

He met her gaze, his eyes knowing.

"I've warned you to stop looking at them as more than what they are. This is the last time I will give you that courtesy."

She lowered her eyes, a stab of fear piercing her chest. It would be so much easier if she didn't come back, just left and started over somewhere that she didn't have to condone the draining of children.

"You just going to stand there?"

Bennet carefully removed the IV drip from the 'donors,' no, the boy, the boy's arm, before wheeling the machine away from the bed as if handling precious crystal. With what was sacred safely set aside, he roughly dragged the boy off the bed, letting his head slam against the metal side rail with a *clang* before dropping him on a gurney.

"What the fuck? Grab the other end! What is with you, Violet?"

Accusations and superiority oozed out of him like a toxic miasma. He wouldn't suffer her much longer; she was freezing up to the point of uselessness.

Violet's hands were slick with sweat, so she grabbed the material piece of the gurney without offering an explanation or excuse, trying to appease him. The air felt warm and humid as they entered the hallway, sweat trickling from her armpits and along her back. Every step felt like another closer to damnation, and she felt short of breath. Was she panicking? After everything she had done and seen, was she finally breaking?

Scorn, guilt, and shame colored her thoughts with vivid splashes of self-loathing, transporting her away from her body to somewhere else. Disassociated, Violet felt nothing as they dumped the boy's body next to a pile of other empty vessels, all haphazardly stacked with little more than toe tags and sheer gowns that exposed their juvenile nakedness, all of them awaiting the incinerator.

For dust thou art, and unto dust shalt thou return.

She let out a little laugh, off-key and bitter, that earned her a reproving stare. Fuck you, fuck you, fuck you, she wanted to shout, but she said nothing.

"I'm going to get a coffee. You coming, or you going to stand around here all night laughing and sweating?"

Eat a dick. "Yeah, alright."

Reality set back in as the door clicked shut behind her. Sparing a glance over her shoulder, she saw the bodies stacked through the window like a human Jenga tower. Her stomach clenched, and she felt like the eyes of God himself were boring into her, damning her for her scriptural jest and her spineless inaction. She's the Nazi who would say, *"I was just following orders,"* as if that could save her from her transgressions.

Violet fell into the chair, her back sliding uncomfortably against its cheap plasticity, still in a daze. Bennet set down a styrofoam cup in front of her and plopped down in the chair opposite, its seat facing away from the table so he could rest his forearms on the chair-back. He slurped the coffee as he turned on the television. Sound blasted out, but Violet didn't react, still seeing the piled children, the toe tags dangling.

What am I doing?

She brought the cup to her lips and could smell the staleness of its contents, souring her stomach.

"Listen, it's been a record-breaking year, and we are very proud of what we've accomplished."

Violet choked on the sip she had just taken, Bennet sparing her an annoyed glance before turning the volume louder.

"With our FDA approval, we can now solidify our amazing gains in eradicating disease and the decaying effect of aging. This is no longer the clinical testing phase Barbara."

Jarum Daughtry's face filled the screen, his *too-perfect* smile mesmerizing and disarming. The screen flashed momentarily to Barbara Finesman, the news anchor interviewing him, and you could see Jarum's natural magnetism's pull on her. She seemed to adore him for just a moment before a resolve sparked in her eyes, and her features cooled. Barbara appeared to be made of firmer stuff.

"While we applaud these milestones for Lazarus, I wanted to ask you about recent allegations of ethical misconduct regarding how you procure your 'donations.' We have recently obtained reports of forced 'donations,' or in other words, forced plasma extraction from people, specifically children, without consent. Do you care to comment?"

Violet took several breaths, trying to suppress the need to cough, transfixed by what was happening; Bennet equally locked in, both of them watching their Chief Executive Officer being confronted with the work they were sworn never to discuss.

She had seen the investor telecasts where Jarum belittled and bullied when he didn't like what he heard. His smile had always remained, but a dark cast would come over his eyes, eerily reminiscent of Ted Bundy's dead stare, evaporating all warmth and warning everyone of what was to come. She saw that same expression on the screen as the camera focused on him, the darkness growing as Babara's question neared completion. Her heart was racing.

He wouldn't lose it on national television, would he?

"That's a fascinating fiction, Barbara. Everything at Lazarus is above board. If it wasn't, do you think the Federal government would have approved our process?"

Violet knew money had exchanged hands, a lot of money. *The FDA never even stepped foot in one of their labs.*

He paused briefly, giving Barbara time to prepare her rebuttal, then continued, stopping her, purposely controlling the narrative so she got the hint of where she belonged in this conversation.

"Now, in the beginning, at the company's founding, we used cells from patients given to us by hospitals to test for reactions, decay, etc. All completely legal based on current laws for obtaining tissue. We understand the implications of historical events, such as the sourcing of the HeLa cells, so we changed tack. All donations are consensual, and we have perfected plasma re-creation so that we now can make a synthetic elixir that no longer requires these donations-"

"Fucking liar," Violet grumbled. Bennet turned to look at her slowly, his eyebrow raised. She felt a bead of sweat roll down her back as she slapped her hand to her mouth, eyes wide. *Why had I said that? Fuck.*

"-der no circumstances would we forcibly take a donation. Period," Jarum was finishing.

Barbara looked at him quizzically, the doubt unveiled and obvious.

"So the allegations of ruthless treatment and rooms filled with, let me see here, the exact phrasing is 'drained bodies ready for the incinerator' are false?"

Jarum scoffed.

"This is utterly ridiculous."

"So is that a 'yes' or a 'no' Mr. Daughtry?"

He glared at her for only a moment before the mask of geniality slipped back into place, but the camera caught that split-second look of hatred—a look of exposure.

A light rumble, as subtle as a flutter, escaped his lips. Laughter.

"So let me guess, America's child abduction problem will be laid at my feet next? Barbara, I think you know better. You are too smart to follow conspiracy theories like this."

Although it wasn't a theory, Violet thought, and she felt bile burn in her throat.

Barbara raised her eyebrow, unmoved or cowed.

Jarum's eyes were ice.

"No."

"Ok," she replied, shifting in her seat, her forehead creased. "What of the reports that some of your patients have developed hallucinatory conditions? We've interviewed several recipients who claim to hear voices, see flashes, and even, and I quote, 'hear buzzing that drowns out all thought.' Is there any validity to that?"

His stare could have frozen the sun.

"If this occurred, it was never brought to the attention of Lazarus. It sounds like a pre-existing condition you opportunistically use to set a particular narrative, Barbara."

Her glare hardened, attempting to rival his. Her head turned ever so slightly.

Violet couldn't help but wonder what was said to her through her earpiece.

She lifted her hands disarmingly, palms out.

"Bygones, Mr. Daughtry. Let's move on. You were sharing one of your success stories with us, right?"

"Back to business, excellent Barbara."

His voice oozed condescension and triumph.

The anchor seemed to whither on screen, seeming less as his personality overpowered the interview, rushing into his success story. An elderly woman with advanced dementia, rejuvenated to the point of wrinkles smoothing, hair growing, and posture straightening. The burden of age being lifted, and all of this covered by Medicare.

"The excitement is more than I can contain, Barbara," he finished jovially, the confrontation seemingly forgotten.

"That is amazing, Mr. Daughtry. And all of this was done with synthetic plasma. Fascinating."

Barbara feigned astonishment, but Violet didn't miss the insincerity. She was enthralled as the train continued, nearing derailment.

"Isn't it?" Jarum's delight was suffused with contempt. "Let me introduce you to her, shall I?"

The camera panned out, taking in the broader stage, several sweaty and harried producers scurrying out of view. An older woman walked past, but her age was hard to determine as she climbed the double stair onto the stage. Her hair and size belonged to someone much older; Sophia Petrillo from the Golden Girls came to Violet's mind, except for her face that was too smooth, obviously so. Her posture was straight, and her movements were of a much younger woman; the swing of her arms, the focus of her sweeping eyes.

Jarum swept his hand with an air of showmanship for the woman to sit. She did so with an off smile, something held back.

"Thank you for joining us, Mrs. Jarlsen-"

"Oh heavens, call me Ruth, Barbara. Excuse me, is Barbara okay?"

"Of course, Ruth." Barbara smiled, something genuine that she wouldn't share with Jarum.

"I am always thrilled when Ruth can join us. Her trans-formation has been miraculous and is exactly why we pursued the 'elixir.'"

Her gaze shifted from Ruth back to Jarum, her eyes scrunching ever so slightly.

"So tell us more. Ruth had dementia, is that right?" After asking, she looked back to Ruth, hoping she would answer, but Jarum continued.

"Precisely and the use of our most advanced plasma treatment not only stopped its progression but also reversed the symptoms, continuing to reverse other aging effects." He shifted his gaze off stage," if you will cue up the old photos."

A side-by-side populated the screen. A picture of a slumped and wrinkled elderly woman juxtaposed against the live view of Ruth sitting on-screen. It was like seeing someone 30 years in the past... almost.

Bennet whistled.

"Wow." Barbara looked genuinely surprised.

"I certainly don't want to question these medical advancements, but can't people use your plasma 'elixir' just cosmetically? How can you or we, the general public, be certain this treatment fixed these advanced medical issues? No offense Ruth, you look wonderful."

Ruth smiled broadly.

"None taken, Barbara. Sorry, Mr. Daughtry, this is my cue. I can remember being forgetful, flashes of my childhood intermixing with the present, often not knowing where I was or when I was. My daughter could attest to this more than I can, being an observer and all, but she's camera shy."

Ruth laughed throatily, and Barbara joined her to keep it congenial.

"Not everyone is comfortable; it took me years," Barbara said.

"Well, I'll be! Huh. Oh, sorry, I'm getting off-topic; totally not cognitively related."

Barbara's smile spread to her eyes, a glint.

"I can tell Ruth... If only this treatment had been around just a few years ago. My mother passed from Alzheimer's."

"I am so sorry to hear that," Jarum said, his look of sympathy unnatural and menacing.

"Thank you."

"To address what you asked earlier, yes, we do have some vintages that are used for cosmetic alterations, but cognitive decline," he shook his head," only an advanced serum that has been reformulated multiple times to hone it for purity and maximum effect, can be used in this instance. We reserve Ambrosh 31 expressly for that."

The room went silent, and Violet stared blankly at the screen.

Ambrosh 31.

Am31.

The girl.

She was half of that blend. That woman, Ruth, has the girl's plasma flowing through her.

Violet stood, knocking the chair over. Bennet muted the TV, turning to her with a scowl.

"Can't you keep it down?"

She flinched.

"Er... Sorry. I gotta go."

"The shift isn't up for another three hours, Vi-"

"I'm not feeling well!"

It was his turn to be startled, both widening their eyes. Violet never shouted, and her hands were shaking.

"Yeah... alright. Get some rest."

"Ok..."

She hurried to her locker, grabbed everything in her arms, and headed toward the elevator, not bothering to zip her bag or pull on her coat.

Am31.

CHAPTER EIGHT

J ulia watched as her mother headed out for another interview, unsure whether to be worried. The change in Ruth came swiftly; her mind clearing and the physical transformation in just five weeks... it was unbelievable. She can't remember the last time she saw her mother stand up straight, bend down without moaning, or even catch something. It was what she hoped for to some degree, but it brought other behaviors she didn't expect.

Ruth demonstrated a hardness and an air of artificiality that Julia doesn't quite remember from before. Her mother was often apt to dress her down, remorselessly treating her like a stupid child if she didn't know something. Ruth had always had an edge before dementia, but this... this was something else.

"And people tell me that I'm the bitch...."

Julia stepped in front of the mirror, applying lipstick and adjusting her shirt. Her mother told her she always had her boobs hanging out like a whore, and she felt self-conscious from the reproach. Her shirt wasn't *that* low cut.

She practiced staring at herself, adjusting the openness of her eyes to perfect a glare of authority. Julia had gotten so used to her mother needing her, so used to being the one running the show for her and her daughter. The reclamation of her mother's self had left her feeling like a boat without a sail, adrift without purpose. Maybe she should date again? It's why she paid several thousand dollars for her own little dose of "elixir," granted without the potency of Ruth's. She just wanted to get rid of her crow's feet.

Julia sighed. When had it become about this? Sagging tits and wrinkles? Worrying about Steve leaving her and then onto the days of her mom calling her names before becoming a hopeless old woman made Julia skip a life step. She forgot to be a woman with needs. Hell, her own daughter was 16 and starting to date, likely getting more than she was.

"Oh fuck, I should probably have that discussion with her," she mumbled.

"Are you talking to yourself?"

Ruth stood behind her, eyebrow raised.

"Apparently."

"No reason to talk back, Julia."

Julia glared at her, mother and daughter fighting an unseen battle for dominance. Ruth tsked but looked away, handing Julia a breadcrumb of victory. She had so little to grapple on to.

"So, how did it go?"

"It was ok. These interviews are getting tiresome. What's the point of getting my life back from the fog if I can't live it?"

Julia nodded in agreement. She knew.

"Mom, I need to ask you something. I've been thinking about this for a while."

Ruth faced her.

"Where were you talking about when you mentioned the fireflies... during your memory journeys?"

That's what Ruth had named them, memory journeys when lucidity slipped through her fingers, and she went somewhere else. Sometime else.

"My childhood home."

"You've never talked about it before."

"I know. It has a lot to be nostalgic for, but... it also holds pain for me, Julia."

"Grandma and Grandpa?"

Ruth nodded, turning toward the mirror to appraise herself.

"Maybe later, ok?"

Julia nodded, giving her mom the moment, attempting to foster goodwill.

"You know what? Let's get Stacie and go to dinner. Enough with this interview stuff. They don't own you, you know."

Ruth stared into the mirror, seeming lost. Was it happening again?

"Mom?"

Ruth's eyes widened in the mirror's reflection like she saw something offstage in a play.

"Wha-"

"Yes, yes, I know, but... oh fuck, why not?" Ruth said, giving her head a subtle shake.

She grabbed her purse and started heading for the door. Julia smiled, hiding her concern and seeking solace in the fact that this was what she had fought for. More time. More life.

She may have thought it would have been an experience with an old lady she had to mother, but this was probably better. This may be their second chance, no matter the challenges and hiccups.

The door opened ahead, and Ruth turned to face her with a glare of impatience.

"Well? Are you coming?"

CHAPTER NINE

Violet screamed, sitting up, phantom breath and fingers still running along her legs and thighs. She inhaled and exhaled, meditatively trying to center herself. The images were so vivid, the sensations so real, but once she woke, they were nothing more than a wisp of smoke from an extinguished candle, faint and fleeting.

"Shit, shit, shit."

She kept repeating the word between her sobs, her eyes clenched out of habit, unsure whether she was trying to keep the dream world in or the real one out. Blackness surrounded her and the silence of her apartment.

Violet finally opened her eyes and blew out several breaths while shaking her hands, trying to recover feeling in them after they'd fallen asleep. She grabbed her phone, her fingers still numb as she tried to get the thumbprint reader to operate.

3:00 AM. The faint *beep* of a heart monitor flexed in her auditory memory. A sharp intake of breath, the death rattle.

"Stop it!" She couldn't silence her demons.

Violet ran to the bathroom, splashing water on her face

to wash away the tears and wake her from her hell, but she wasn't dreaming. Her consciousness was betraying her.

Something unrecognizable looked out from the mirror; red eyes set in a puffy face, lined with too many worry lines for her age.

Please.

"I'm sorry..." Her whisper answered. The pleas were what plagued her. Not just those of the children's toe-tags flashing through her mind; the jumble of bodies—but also her patients from when she made a difference or tried to.

The small hand reached for the material of her pant leg, drifting across without the strength to grasp.

Her brother. The first patient she'd ever lost. He was unearthed from within.

He'd always been sickly, it's the reason she chose to go to medical school, but leukemia came on quickly and savagely, decimating his body like a wildfire consumed kindling.

She had him admitted to her hospital, to her ward. She had promised she'd help him, promised her parents and herself, but each treatment was no more effective than a trickle of water on the conflagration.

Vi... help-p...

The sorrow flowed down her cheeks, the dam in her heart finally burst, releasing a deluge of emotion on all planes of her being.

A deep inhalation. A gasp.

"I'm sorry-"

The tears were torrential, a cleansing of her soul. Each tear surfaced another memory: Little league. Christmas. Babysitting. First steps. Bike jumps. Watching Hocus Pocus. She wiped each one away, her shoulders a bit lighter with each swipe of her hand. Looking in the mirror at the ragged creature before her once more, she saw it. Beneath the guilt and the shame, a glint of recognition. Violet was still there.

"Goddammit. I'm coming."

Rolling her shoulders back, she took a deep breath and exhaled. She couldn't just sit back any longer. That malleable part of her hardened, that piece she let Lazarus mold and manipulate. Their promises were everything she wished had existed for her brother, everything she dreamed she could help bring to the world: to never let another suffer her family's loss, the death of a child.

They'd come at the opportune time, at the coattails of her devastation, and sold her what they could build together if she joined; what they ultimately built together. She saw the miracles; she witnessed them, but the dark truth of their origin...

Each new day brought another expiring child, and Violet buried her brother deeper and deeper beneath layers of shame and hypocrisy that her dreams wouldn't let her escape. How had she allowed herself to become so far gone? How could she let a loved one become nothing more than a figment of shattered memory, a pane of consciousness in which she cast stones to justify her complicity?

No more.

She finished dressing and reached the door with a renewed sense of calm she hadn't felt in a long time. A small hand seemed to clasp over hers as she grabbed the knob and turned, giving her strength.

Stay with me, Brian, she thought and stepped over the threshold.

CHAPTER TEN

The floor was quiet. No beeping. No mechanical reverberations of refrigeration systems. Nothing.

He leaned back in the chair, multiple monitors flashing between one room's surveillance to another, and he took a deep breath. The calm was becoming less frequent. Donors had started expiring at an accelerated rate as of late, and Violet, acting like a lunatic, endangering their lives, started talking to that damn donor. Violet knew better. How could she do this?

Violet had always had a soft spot for their charges, showing the compassion one would expect from her sex, but that black girl, Am31... there is something about her. Bennet couldn't take the risk.

I should take care of her while it's just me here. She's endangering everything.

His eyebrow lifted, pondering and full of indecision. This wouldn't be the first time he forced nature's hand with a donor, but he'd always had other reasons unrelated to self-preservation.

He tapped the enter key, and the screen switched to a

hospital room. Everything was white and sterile, bed centered with the girl stark against the homogeneity, looking from side to side, lost. It would be so easy.

The sheet moved in fits and spurts; her body racked with inconsistent tremors, eyes wide.

She shivered, wracked with convulsions... Bennet twitched, hitting enter again to cut the feed, his sigh like a howling wind in the silence.

"Fuck it, whatever."

He took a sip of his coffee, cold and stale, solely for the utility of finishing his shift.

'Daddy,' the girl cried out, voice quivering as her body continued to seize.

Bennet rubbed his eyes, trying to massage it away, but the images wouldn't leave, a ghost haunting his conscience.

His hands slammed the desk, his body moving of its own accord. The hallway moved past as if in a dream, him being a spectator to someone else's life. His rounds usually helped, the walking a distraction from what he needed to do or, more often, what he already had, but that girl had rattled him. *Violet* had rattled him. Why couldn't she leave well enough alone? All that he had to do... it's not like-

Clang

A door slammed in the distance, the sound reverberating through the halls like the striking of a cymbal. Events had started to move too fast, a turning point Bennet had missed with the arrival of that girl.

He walked faster, feet moving him toward Am31's room before he even realized it. 38B, he could see it just ahead, its edges blurred like he was in a trance.

She needs to die.

As Bennet approached, a figure came into focus, emerging from the intersecting hallway. They moved quickly, hand on the handle, ready to enter the room. Nobody else should have been there.

"Hey, what the fuck do you think you're doing?" He said.

The figure swiveled to face him, body tense like a startled cat.

Violet.

She stood in front of him, frozen, face a mix of shock and determination. Their eyes met, and he braced himself, unsure of her next move. Violet was supposed to be at home, unable to finish the day. Why had she come back?

Then the puzzle piece fell into place; she'd returned for the girl.

Violet withered as he stiffened his posture, trying to intimidate her, but she held her ground despite cowering, fear in her eyes. The door swung inward; her hand clutched tight around the handle.

"I know why you are here," he said, stepping forward.

"Please, you never saw me," her voice was high, but she wasn't cowed.

"I can't let you do this, Violet. It's agains-"

"Who do you fucking owe?" She asked, voice harder and laced with anger.

"They murder children. Is that what you want on your conscience, Bennet? Is it? Being the lap dog to corporate fascists?"

"Enough! You better watch your mouth."

She stood straighter, finding her mettle.

"Or you'll kill me too? Isn't that how this goes? I- I can't be a party to this anymore... I just can't."

Bennet reached out to grab her, but she was faster, swinging her free arm around and slamming something into his neck. His body convulsed, and he could hear the door bang shut as his body shuddered on the ground.

'Daddy,' her voice was hoarse, tears wetting the collar of her shirt. The girl's body was still, inhumanly so, after the violent tremors from moments before. The girl tried to lift her hand, and it fell to her side, a sudden snap like the cutting of the puppet's strings. Her mouth opened and was silent.

Bennet gasped, catching his breath, his eyes wide, brow damp.

She fucking tased me.

Rolling onto his side, he crawled away from the room, slowly reaching his feet.

'Daddy.'

He clenched his eyes shut, tears dripping down while the occasional tremor still wracked his body.

"No, no, no, no, no," he said, gripping his ears, trying to seal out the words.

Bennet felt something break inside; he thought he could hear the crack.

He ran.

Clang, clang, clang, each door went as he moved from room to room, looking to escape the ghost at his heels.

The air was heavy in the early morning dew, the only light from the overhead phosphorescents guiding his way in a labyrinth of darkness.

Daddy-

"No-" he cut off as everything went dark.

CHAPTER ELEVEN

The light was blazing, a white glare blotting out the horizon. Lavender, stronger than before, seemed to dance with the honeysuckle at each breath, overwhelming her senses; taste and smell. She could feel the grass beneath her fingers, dewy and lush, tickling her arms and jutting between her fingers.

"Mama?"

The light receded as footsteps reached her ears, gentle and swift. The cabin rested in the distance, squat and familiar, as two women stood apart mere feet from one another and beckoned to her, seemingly unaware of the other. One of them was Mama, thin and determined, exuding her will against her visitor, an older woman, yet ageless, face wreathed in fireflies.

"Mama, what do I do?" she yelled, her vocal cords raw.

Her mother's hand extended, and her eyes flashed, pulling her daughter into her orbit like a black hole, forcing the pulses of the other woman away.

"Kami, baby, come to me."

She pulled herself upright, thrusting her arms forward,

stretching as much as she could, flailing and reaching for her mother's fingers. They came so close, what seemed like inches, a humming white noise building to a crescendo in her ears.

"A little more, baby. Ka-"

"-m31. Am31, you have to wake up. Come on."

Kami's eyes opened, and the bright light remained, but the periphery was sterile metal and tile, the chocolate features of her mother fading into the paleness of the doctor. All but her eyes, green flecked with brown. Kind-eyes, she needed to trust her.

"You came back."

Kami didn't even recognize her voice, raw and phlegmy, a sound more like a gargle than anything else.

The woman winced before nodding.

"I am going to get you out of here. We don't have much time, and we can talk later. They will kill us both once they notice, once they see."

Kind-eyes nodded her head toward the camera in the corner of the room, its circular lens as dangerous as a bullseye.

Kami nodded, her whole body shaking as she tried to move her legs to the edge of the bed.

"Too... weak."

Her breath was labored as she tried to move, not knowing how long it had been since she'd moved that far, tremors rattling the bedside bar as she grabbed it.

"Name..." she asked in little more than a whisper.

"Violet."

"I'm Kami."

Violet stared back at Kami, a recognition passing over like the noonday sun, and for the first time, Kami felt seen, as if those words stripping away her number made her the real person she was again. Violet nodded, eyes glistening with tears, acknowledging what Kami had sensed.

"Ok, Kami, let's get out of here."

The process was slow as Kami moved in fits and starts, like an infant taking its first steps, and after several minutes, Violet supported her as they opened the door to the room.

"I'm not sure how far I can make it at this rate. Let me-"

"No. Don't leave me here again."

Kami's voice recovered a bit of its strength.

"I was just going to find a wheelchair."

"I'd rather crawl than be left here to be put back."

Violet nodded, feeling the chill in Kami's voice, and started walking. Kami's feet made a thud with each step, panic rising ever more steadily to the surface.

Thud, thud

The sound was like gunshots in the silence. Someone would hear and stop them. She felt the sweat dripping down her back and under her arms, making her shirt slide under Violet's grip.

"Whoa," slipped from her lips as she slid to the ground, her legs still rubbery beneath her weight, despite her diminished frame.

Violet knelt next to her.

"Are you ok? I'm sorry. Look, you just aren't strong enough. We are halfway to the exit. I'm grabbing a wheelchair."

Kami's eyes went wide with panic as she clawed at Violet's sleeve but to no avail. She was too winded to yell after her, but she couldn't stay.

They can't retake me!

She slid forward, her movements sloppy and frantic,

but she refused to give them another opportunity. She'd rather die. *Mama! Shawn! Somebody help me!*

Thud, thud

Thud, thud

Thud, thud

Her body bounced down the hallway, elbows and knees banging against the ground like a dragged corpse. She could hear nothing but her advance and prayed she would make it.

A door slammed in the distance, and she froze. Cold sweat ran from her brow, and her breaths came out in wheezes.

A wheel squeaked in a constant rhythm, the cyclical dread drawing closer with each rotation.

Kami jolted, almost unconsciously, moving forward even faster, her elbows raw beneath her smock from the constant rubbing of each movement. She could see the doorway up ahead, so close yet so far. She would make it. She would-

A hand grabbed the back of her shirt, and she spun, hissing like a feral cat, losing all sense of reality outside survival.

"Hey, hey! Kami, it's me. Stop, stop, it's ok," Violet pleaded as she batted away Kami's arms and embraced her, holding her tight as she wept.

"Shhh, it's ok. I told you I was getting a chair. I won't leave you. Shhh now. You're safe."

The words were hollow to Kami for what was safety, yet she couldn't help feeling the sincerity from Violet, as if she really believed they were, or perhaps, would be.

Several minutes passed before the shaking stopped enough that Violet could guide her into the wheelchair. The door was just ahead, but what awaited them outside those doors? How could Kami have thought she could do anything out there?

"Ready?" Violet asked.

Kami nodded, her eyes heavy with exhaustion, the adrenaline finally running its course.

Violet gave her hand a squeeze before pushing forward and taking them outside.

CHAPTER TWELVE

His head ached, red sticky blood matting his hair where he had hit the pavement. Everything was moving so quickly, control slipping out of his fingers. Did he even care?

Jarum was the devil; Bennet knew that. Never would such a miracle cure come along without payment, even if it wasn't monetary. He had sold his soul so long ago and knew Violet had done something similar. That's why he thought he could trust her. But at what point was enough truly enough?

He staggered to his feet, flash memories of his daughter's seizures gripping him at each breath. Every donor that expired was a mark on his soul that he buried beneath layers of guilt. The waxy faces. The lifeless eyes... but his daughter's, they still had life. That had to justify this.

Bang

The door to the complex slammed shut as a figure pushing a wheelchair ran across the parking lot. He knew it was Violet with the girl.

"I need you to keep an eye on things for me—nothing

extreme, of course, but just as a thank you for your daughter. Keep things running smoothly around here as payment for her treatment, and we'll call it even. What do you say, Bennet?"

Jarum's words floated in his consciousness as if spoken anew, a threat conveyed as only Jarum would. Bennet ground his teeth.

"Quickly now, get in. I got you."

Violet's voice was harried, the strain visible on her face even in the faint overhead lights. There was no surprise when her eyes met his as he grabbed her wrist, Am31 screaming as if stabbed.

"I already warned you to leave me alone," Violet said, defiant and weary.

"No," Bennet said.

"Or what, B? You going to hurt me? Add me to the pile with the children?"

He winced; her words had teeth.

"You don't understand. Do you think I like doing this? Sometimes you have to swallow what you want for something greater?"

Violet sucked in air, face aghast.

"I've fucking swallowed it, a poison pill that's killing me and everyone else. Nothing is worth this. I can't look the other way anymore-"

"My daughter!"

And then she understood, recognition lighting her eyes.

They weren't all that different, doing what they knew to be wrong with the ideal of helping those they loved or lost with the promise that others wouldn't have to suffer the same way they had. Violet didn't know the exact deal Bennet made but finally understood there were stakes, and she could respect him for that. She also knew he felt he didn't have a choice.

She nodded.

"Bennet, I'm sorry...."

The tension that had been rippling in his shoulders and face finally loosened. For the first time, there was tenderness in his eyes.

"I can't let you."

"I know," she said, and before he could react, she swung her arm, the scalpel slicing cleanly through flesh, leaving a veil of blood from the wound beneath his jawline.

"Now you don't have to."

He slumped, releasing her and clutching his throat, trying to hold it all in. The pavement came rushing to meet him, and Bennet's last thoughts were of his daughter walking again before his wife discovered the true price for her recovery. They were finally free.

CHAPTER THIRTEEN

"I want you home by ten, Stacie; I mean it. Yes, I love you too. Ok, bye, sweetie."

Julia hung up the phone, and Ruth watched her over her wine glass, the daughterly exchange she had so many times with Julia not lost on her.

Reflecting on it, so much of her life was a blur. No matter what recovery she made due to Lazarus, no tincture can ever truly bring back every memory. Disease or not, life moves by in flashes, moments of beauty lost among the monotony, with great peaks of joy and trauma being the only still-life that remains in the mind's eye.

Ruth tipped the glass back, feeling the burn of the Merlot in her throat, giving her stomach a momentary clench, and a flutter of yellow dots danced across her vision.

She eyed the waiter as he walked past and pointed to her glass. His posture stiffened, and he turned quickly toward the bar with a nod.

She closed her eyes, the blackness engulfing her while the hum of the restaurant pulsed around her, the lights flickering as if to the beat of wings. The fireflies. She sucked in air, unable to catch her breath as the darkness pulled on her.

"-om! Mom!"

Ruth felt the squeeze, and her eyes opened with an indescribable force, the simple act of blinking feeling like the release of a spring.

Julia held her arm, forehead scrunched in alarm, eyes wide.

Ruth cleared her throat.

"Julia, don't frown, or you'll need Botox, and the money you spent on that elixir would have been for nothing."

"Are you fucking kidding me right now. You were hyperventilating, Mom. Tell me what is going on."

The waiter hesitantly approached and set the glass in front of Ruth, who grasped it before his fingertips left the stem. Julia was just as fast.

"I didn't take care of you all these years and seek a cure so you can become a drunk. Hands off the glass, old woman. I mean it."

Ruth, startled, sat back against her chair, posture stiffening.

"Watch your mouth."

"Then tell me what is happening, Mom. What's going on with you?"

"Julia, I think you've worried about me long enough, okay? Everything going on, it's... it's just a lot to process. How long ago was it that I was on my way to the looney bin for old ladies, and now," she raised her hands along her silhouette and stopped at her breasts," I look like I'm in my forties again. This isn't natural. I'm thankful, but there is so much I can't...."

"You can't what?"

"Do you remember your childhood?"

"My child- what are you talking about, Mom?"

"Answer the question, Julia."

"Yes, I remember my childhood."

"All of it?"

"Well, not every detail but the important things. Nobody remembers everything."

Ruth looked at her hands. They were young, but she could feel the tremor of age beneath the surface, an insidious serpent waiting in the brush to strike its victim.

"I remember parts of mine in sharp relief, like a movie playing before my eyes, but it's wrong. Tainted. And your childhood, my middle life, is still a blur. There are parts that I can see as flashes like Stacie being born, but most..." she closes her eyes, and the fireflies flicker in her periphery.

Julia places her hand back on her mother's, gently this time, and gives it a squeeze. Ruth meets her gaze, settling into their pools of concern.

"Should we talk to someone? I think Lazarus has done enough. I'm talking about a therapist. You are like someone who just came out of a years-long coma. I can't even-"

"No."

Julia released her mother's hand, surprised by the firmness in her voice.

"But Mom, I just-"

"Did I stutter? I said no."

Julia exhaled and sat back in her chair. She didn't know how to reach her. Her mother had always been stubborn, often mean as she aged, but she could be reasoned with on the important stuff. Since Lazarus, though, the hardness had become more frequent.

Ruth lifted her glass to her lips and took a sip, savoring it.

"Is this about the fireflies again? The cabin? Grandma and Grandpa?"

Ruth set the glass down and stared back at Julia. They stared at one another, assessing and not the challenge either expected.

A tear escaped Ruth's eye, leaving a faint trail down her smooth cheek. She lowered her gaze, and Julia felt she'd won the battle she didn't know they were waging, and she felt remorse for it.

"There's a girl I see. She's there."

"She's where?" Julia's voice was soft, barely above a whisper to match her mother's.

"The cabin. She's so bright, Julia. Like trying to look at a star, and I'm so dark. The fireflies keep attaching to me. They are consuming me, but she, she shines. She won't rescue me."

"Is this a recurring dream?"

Ruth looked up, startled.

"This is no dream," she said, her voice so full of conviction that no rational person would doubt her, yet Julia was puzzled. Nothing her Mom said made any sense.

"Okay, okay, Mom. But what is she rescuing you from?"

"Them…"

Julia looked around the restaurant. People surrounded them, faces full of joy or monotony, contentment, and restlessness; the sights of life. Laughter and conversation buzzed around them, but nobody paid them any mind. They were alone, their table an island.

She looked back at her mother who seemed to shrink before her, the new polished veneer cracking under the weight.

"Who?"

"It doesn't matter. Mama keeps pulling at her light. She's going to her."

"Mama? Is that supposed to be Grandma?"

"No, Julia, I," Ruth took another sip of her wine and then pushed the glass away.

"I want to find the cabin."

Julia nodded, frowning.

"Yeah, Mom, okay. We'll find the cabin, but first, I think-"

"We need to leave now, Julia. I know you think I've lost my mind, and frankly, I have too, but something is happening, and I need to do this. I need," she took a deep breath before continuing," I need your help."

Julia sighed and then nodded slowly, taking her phone out.

"I'll call Steve, the least he can do is watch his daughter for a night or two. Then we can go."

Ruth sucked in a loud breath and grabbed her daughter's hand. Julia met her eyes, urgent and expectant.

"Thank you."

CHAPTER FOURTEEN

T he sun set behind them as the cars rushed by, the sky purple like a deep bruise and the plethora of headlights twinkling like stars in the twilight.

They'd been driving for hours, Violet unsure of where she was going, but Kami seemed to know. When she first mentioned the cabin, Violet agreed immediately, seeing the iron-clad determination of the girl. Confidence that, despite weeks of captivity, hadn't wavered.

She also knew that they were likely being tracked. It took her the first two hours of driving as the sun rose to remember the tracker embedded in Kami's skin, which was inserted into every "donor" as soon as they reached the facility, but what was the range of it? How soon would somebody be onto them?

Violet's face would be splashed across the company's internal bulletins; the camera stills full of her assisting the girl out of the facility.

"Mmm"

Gasp

Kami convulsed and shivered before her breathing

steadied, still asleep. She had done this multiple times, the first causing Violet to pull over and check her vitals, only for Kami to wake up, swatting her away. The girl would likely have nightmares like this for years, if not the rest of her life, besides never being able to trust Violet or anyone else. She didn't blame her. How could Violet have been a part of this?

Her stomach churned with the shame of it. She had sacrificed everything she had promised herself, all her morals, and for what? The greater good? That was clearly something open to interpretation. She blinked away tears as she pulled off the highway.

A neon sign blazed in the darkness for a gas station, the only sign of life for miles, and a lone attendant watched them wearily pull in from behind cloudy glass.

"Where are we?" Kami asked, eyes puffy and thick with sleep.

"We just need some gas. Go back to sleep."

She started to insert her card and pulled it out quickly. If the tracker wasn't working, this would for sure let them know she was here.

"Fuck," she whispered.

"Hey, I'm going to run in quick to pay," she said, looking through the car window to Kami, who nodded, her face apprehensive.

The gas station had a thick, mildew smell, and the attendant eyed her suspiciously.

"$20, please."

Violet slid the bill under the glass divider, and the woman nodded to her.

"Thank you," she said and turned to leave.

Creak

She missed a step, nearly stumbling over her own feet.

There didn't appear to be anyone else in the building;

her car was the only one in the lot. She gave a half smile to the woman behind the counter and felt sweat trickle down her back.

The woman stared back at her, her gaze switching from cautious to hard and predatory. Violet noticed her hand was illuminated and heard the soft vibration of a phone.

Shit.

She continued back to the car, her pace quickening while trying not to draw attention to herself. Kami watched her, eyes wide. She could tell something wasn't right.

Violet started fueling and gestured for Kami to start the car. Shadows danced in the flickering overhead lights. The attendant stood in the window, watching.

She got back in the car, and a man exited the gas station, walking in their direction.

"Shit!"

"Go!" Kami yelled almost at the same time.

The tires squealed as they sped forward, turning in a tight circle. The side window shattered as a bullet punched through it.

"They found us! How did they find us?"

"Just hold on!"

They swung out onto the street precariously, the back of the car fishtailing and missing a black SUV that sped past, all of its lights off. The red brake lights flashed angrily in the darkness, accompanying the screeching of the tires on the damp pavement.

"Oh my god, they tried to hit us. Drive faster!"

Violet clenched the steering wheel as she pushed her foot to the floor, swerving back onto the onramp, barely in control.

"Where are we going? I have to know."

"The cabin, I can feel it."

"We have to cut the tracker out of you. I thought they were far enough away, but we can't hide like this."

Kami stared at her, eyes furrowed, and her lips curled in a snarl.

"What the hell are you talking about?"

"There is a tracker that was injected into your right forearm. I didn't know how it worked precisely, but we'd been driving for hours, and they were here. In the middle of nowhere. They're tracking you."

Kami looked down at her arm and started rubbing it. Within seconds her hand tensed into a claw and began scratching at her arm, furiously trying to scratch away her skin.

"I want to be free!" Tears rolled down her cheeks, a child that suffered more than any adult could bear.

Violet clasped one of her hands over Kami's to still the self-inflicted onslaught.

"It's here, but don't hurt yourself like this. We'll make it."

Violet traced a tiny bump on the backside of her forearm, equidistant between the elbow and the wrist.

"Give me something. A knife. Anything!"

Violet looked at Kami and felt a twinge of fear at the calmness in her voice, a solidity that didn't hide her anger but enhanced it. The shackles of civilized obedience and restraint had been stripped away.

The engine whined furiously as Violet nodded and pressed the accelerator to the floor.

"My bag at your feet should have some medical supplies. There should be something in there you can use."

Her voice quivered at the last, but she kept her eyes forward. She needed to be as hard as Kami; she couldn't falter for the girl's sake.

Gauze and packets spilled onto Kami's feet with the loud crinkling of plastic as she rifled through the bag. Her pace was one of determination.

She sat upright and held out her arm.

"What did you find?" Violet asked.

"Just a pair of scissors. We wouldn't be so lucky to have something sharp like a knife."

Violet flinched, remembering the scalpel. She had to move fast. Bennet's blood on her fingers...

"Can you-"

"I have this. Just drive."

Violet heard Kami suck in air and moan as she pushed the scissor point into her skin. The girl bent over, pushing harder and whimpering.

"Kami-"

"Just focus on the road."

Her voice was strained but determined. She wasn't going to stop.

Violet felt heat rise in her cheeks. She could have helped this girl, yet her every decision had caused her pain. She had to do more.

The car swerved from one lane to the next, the constant purr of the engine becoming deafening.

Rest Stop 1 Mile

"Hold on, Kami."

"J-just drive," she said, voice strained.

"But-"

"Here, now just... ugh, just drive."

Kami held out her hand. A puddle of blood pooled in her palm, a small square circuit floating atop it.

Violet met her eyes. Tears welled and rolled down her face, but the hardness and resolve were bright, like a lighthouse stubbornly piercing the fog.

Blood flowed from her arm, a jagged lightning-shaped incision etching her arm.

"Jesus, Kami!"

Grabbing the chip from her hand, Violet rolled down the window and tossed it outside before jerking the wheel hard to the right. The screech of tires and blaring horns erupted as she just made the exit for the rest stop, turning off her headlights and praying nothing would walk out in front of them.

She stood on the brake to bring them to a stop, partially hidden from view behind a semi-truck.

Her hands moved robotically, tearing through gauze and disinfectant packets as she treated the wound.

"Stay still, ok? Hold this here."

She clasped Kami's hand around a thick gauze, hoping she would maintain consciousness long enough for her to stitch the wound.

Sweat dripped from her forehead onto her hands in the stuffy confines of the car as she pierced Kami's skin, trying to stitch as quickly as possible, her grip getting slick.

"I'm almost done. Stay awake."

Violet could see pressure from Kami's hand lightening, her face growing pale.

Each beat of her heart was another loop finished, swift strokes ending what seemed an eternity in a dozen thunderous rhythms.

"They won't get me...."

Kami leaned back against the seat, the fight leaving her.

Violet's hands shook as the adrenaline wore off. Wiping the blood from her hands, she faced forward, surveying the parking lot in the moonlight.

"Where are we going?"

"To Mama... drive."

CHAPTER FIFTEEN

L ights shimmered, blinking in and out of the darkness like stars in a cloud-filled sky. The pulses were bright yellow; caution.

The blackness drank in the sound, the quiet so stark it was deafening, as the lights summoned a buzzing that muffled all thought.

Flash, buzz

Abyss

Flash, buzz

Abyss

The cadence increased; strobe lights of yellow melted into a solid brightness that rivaled the sun; all the while, the buzzing hummed like a power generator, growing ever closer.

"Wake."

A sharp inhalation startled Julia as she drove down the gravel driveway, causing her to slam on the brakes.

Ruth was taking deep breaths, fighting with her seatbelt.

"Mom!"

Ruth's head snapped to face Julia, her eyes glassy and wide. She could never remember this level of fear, even during her lapses.

"What is it? What's wrong?"

Julia could hear the panic in her voice, and she chided herself for it. She needed to remain calm, or this would only get worse. She knew how to handle her mother like this, but she just didn't think she'd have to do so again so soon.

"Julia?"

Ruth's eyes began to clear, the fog melting before the light of lucidity.

The seatbelt quivered as her hands clutched it tightly, her knuckles white.

"Take a breath, Mom. It's ok. We're in the car. I'm right here next to you."

Ruth nodded, resigned as she pawed at the seatbelt. Julia grasped her hand in hers and felt it loosen. She didn't let go.

"Should I keep going? The cabin is just ahead."

"Yes."

Her voice was hoarse, barely more than a whisper.

Gravel crunched as the car lurched forward to the end of the driveway. The cabin was dark, faintly lit by the unmasked moon above. Nothing stirred but the sparse cattails dotting the clearing.

Ruth took a deep breath.

"Ok. We should go inside."

Julia eyed her mother wearily. She knew nothing of this

place, and the idea of breaking and entering wasn't exactly what she expected to take place.

"Um, Mom-"

"Julia, please."

She sighed in acquiescence and stepped out of the car. The air was thick and wet, a blanket of humidity that clung to every surface. Julia could feel the sweat beading down her back, yet her trepidation also had something to do with it.

What were they doing there?

Ruth approached the cabin gingerly, like a fawn testing its wobbly legs for the first time. She was shaken, unsure of her thoughts. She began to wonder if the treatment had worn off, feeling the hardening of age within her. She felt like the sun-baked soil in the desert, cracked and crumbled.

"Mom, let me help you."

Julia grabbed her hand and walked in lockstep, perspiration building between their interlocked fingers.

Buzz

The sound reverberated through Ruth's state of consciousness. Her vision blurred as the bright yellow sun flared in her mind, overcoming her sight.

"Mom, it's ok. You're hurting my hand. Relax, I'm here."

Julia's face materialized with Ruth's strained inhalation. They were in the doorway, fireflies dancing in the dark open field as the scent of hay and lilac tickled her nose.

Her daughter looked frightened, but she wore a mask of bravery. Ruth had been able to do that once. She could still muster that courage.

"Let's go in."

CHAPTER SIXTEEN

Kami could feel the pull toward the cabin, like a rope tied to her heart, luring her in. Mama would be there. Kami could sense it. She dreamt of her. She was so bright, a star glowing with unveiled intensity, but that woman kept trying to eclipse her. The woman with no face, just a void crowned with shimmering fireflies blazing with malevolence.

It was all so confusing to her, yet precise in its imagery. Mama was alive, but someone or something was trying to blot her out.

The car swerved, and she opened her eyes. Violet was hunched over the wheel, her head shaking as she tried to wake herself. They wouldn't make it much further if she didn't rest soon, but there wasn't time. Kami needed to keep her focused on the path and moving ahead.

Violet may have come back for her, but could she really trust this woman who watched her drained of her life, drugged, and tortured?

Kami clenched her hand harder on the pair of scissors in her pocket, the ones Violet lost sight of as she worried over the crater Kami had dug into her arm, fishing for that tracker.

She just needed to get to Mama and things would be normal again. Maybe she could find Shawn and could go back to the way things were, watching him play basketball with the boys and sneaking kisses in the alley on their way home.

She rubbed her lips as she felt the ghost of his on hers that last time before he vanished. Before her whole life got turned upside down.

The road felt rougher as gravel banged about in the wheel wells, shaking her back to the present. They were so close now; Mama was just around that next turn... but so was the other woman. So was the darkness.

How was she there? What would she find once they arrived?

"Hey..."

"Hmm?" Violet said, turning to face her. Her eyes looked hollow in the glow of the dashboard lights.

"It's just up ahead. Once we get there, we can rest."

"Are you sure? I can't go much further."

"I know. Yeah, turn right there."

Violet slowed down to look for her turnoff. The sky was clear, illuminating everything in the moonlight, but nothing else was around. This would be a perfect place to hide a body if they were still being followed. Kami shivered at that thought.

She bounced hard, knocking her head on the side window as Violet made the turn, almost missing it.

"Ow!"

"Sorry, it's so dark."

Kami rubbed her head and looked forward through the

windshield. A flash of light, like a flare, burst forth in front of her.

"She's up ahead, hurry!"

"Wha... um, ok."

Violet's voice was flat and disbelieving, her eyes little more than slits. She didn't have the energy for anything else.

Radiance shined like something Kami had never seen before. The warmth, it was her Mama, calling for her.

Come home, baby

Shadows began to creep out of her periphery, eating the light, drinking it up as if through a straw along the edges. She wouldn't lose her mother's light. She couldn't.

"No!" Kami yelled, covering her face with her hands.

"What?" Violet slammed on the brakes wide-eyed, staring at Kami. "What is it?"

Kami looked at her.

"You couldn't see it?"

"See what?"

"The light."

"It's dark. That's all I see. We're here; should we not be?"

Kami dropped her hands, sitting upright, breath quickening.

There was a car in the driveway.

CHAPTER SEVENTEEN

Dishes sat on the counter, and the air smelled like fried oil. It was fresh like somebody had just finished cooking. They weren't alone.

Ruth cringed with every step, the buzzing of the fireflies swiveling from ear to ear, challenging her sense of direction.

"So this is it?" Julia asked, eyebrows raised with a hint of dismissal in her voice.

Ruth thought a little wonderment would have been nice, but her fear smothered any indignation that bubbled beneath the surface.

Julia took a few steps toward Ruth, each slow and deliberate, like walking on hot coals. She was just as uncomfortable as Ruth.

"Mom, someone has been living here. I think it would be best for us to go. We don't need any trouble."

"I can't go yet."

Her voice was firm. Julia opened her mouth to refute but thought better of it.

Wafts of something flowery and sweet swirled in the

air, mixing with the musk and staleness that greeted them when they entered, a flutter of life that seemed at odds with the dark room.

Water dripped in the sink, and shadows stretched across the single couch in the center of the room.

Ruth's anger flared.

She was here. This illusion of stillness was all wrong. She could sense her, smell her.

"Where the fuck are you? I know you are in here."

Ruth stomped her foot as the volume of her voice escalated.

"You haunt my dreams, terrorizing me at every turn, and now you won't face me. I can't sleep. I can't live. I've had enough. Stop hiding, you coward!"

A rattling came from behind her as the buzzing increased with her anger.

Light flared before her, paralyzing her like a deer entranced by headlights.

Buzz

Buzz

Buzz

Ruth's scream finally shattered the bombardment, and as she blinked away the tears, she realized she had fallen, Julia standing over her.

"Oh, thank god. Come on, let me help you."

Her daughter was kneeling next to her and helped her sit up.

"Wha-" she broke off as she noticed the woman in scrubs standing in the doorway with a young black girl. *The* black girl... the other in the dream whose eyes always smoldered.

"Where's Mama?" The girl said, a bloody pair of scissors in her hand, pointed at Ruth.

She got to her feet and matched the girl's stare.

"Who the hell are you?"

"Don't you ever talk to my baby like that."

Everyone turned to the back of the cabin, and stepping out of the shadows was Kami's Mama.

CHAPTER EIGHTEEN

"Where the fuck are they?" Jarum Daughtry asked, sitting regally behind his desk. His words were slow and over-articulated, anger seething just below the surface.

"I- I don't know, sir. The tracker went offline in Pennsylvania right after our team couldn't apprehend them."

"Leave."

His glare was unnerving, pupils small as pinpricks, unblinking. They were inhuman.

The security technician backed out of the room, afraid to lose sight of him.

Jarum turned his gaze back to the tablet on his desk, looping the security footage of his employee helping Am31 before confronting Bennet in the parking lot and slicing his throat. The gall of that woman. He had worked much too hard for the story of that girl to get out, and they would have to be dealt with no matter the cost.

A surge of rage coursed through him, and the broken halves of the tablet materialized in his clenched hands.

"Fuck."

The shattering of glass chimed as a precursor to the knock on his door, pieces of the device splayed across the floor.

Jarum was standing, frames of consciousness skipping a beat in his rage.

"What?"

The door moved a fraction.

"Sir, is everything alright?"

The voice at the door was shaky and meek—just another pathetic sycophant with nothing of value to add.

"What do you think? Where is Hotchkins? Tell him to get in here now."

"Y-yes, sir. He just arrived."

The door flew open, and Kenny walked in, taking a seat across from Jarum with a sense of ease that nobody else would dare display in front of him, but their history made it impossible for him not to. Wherever Jarum went, Kenny followed, always the mouthpiece for whatever Jarum envisioned; his very own Goebbels.

That level of trust and their intimacy granted such confidence. Besides, Jarum would never get rid of his public relations thermometer and truth sayer just because he didn't quake when Jarum glared at him for putting his feet on his desk. What they had been was no longer a factor.

"We have to contain this, Kenny."

"I agree, but we need to approach this carefully. Too much has been leaking lately, and we have already heard rumors of suspected ruthlessness by the company and you in the media."

Jarum slammed his fists into the desk.

"Ruthlessness? What do they mean by ruthlessness? What company ever became great without a little sacrifice? What would have come about without the Tuskegee Experiment or the culturing of the HeLa cells? What is this pious crusading everybody is on? Or is this just a direct repudiation of my character? The greatest innovators in technological history were ruthless. I am the Steve-fucking-Jobs of the biotech industry, and I will be respected, god dammit!"

Kenny released an audible sigh, not bothering to make eye contact.

"Are you done?"

Jarum sat slowly, inhaling and exhaling quickly, almost to the point of hyperventilation. He opened his eyes and smiled, the artificial edge poking through the surface. It was a pantomime display with no warmth. Any animal would sense the danger.

"Yes, I am."

"Good, because I can't contain this unless we figure out how to staunch the leak. I need you level-headed on this, Jarum."

Kenny was sitting upright now, earnest, his finely tailored clothing wrinkled and puffy dark circles anchoring his brooding eyes. How did Jarum miss this? Their facade was beginning to wear.

"The vultures are circling, and we are teetering on the edge of being exposed and collapsing. We've done so much good, but we both know at what cost we achieved this. People care, Jarum. Now, I can spin this, but we need to make damn sure these escapees are dealt with. She gave us plenty of ammo with her graphic throat cut to spin mental instability, but anything we say can backfire until we know they are contained."

"How long have you been worried about this, Kenny?"

Kenny's brow furrowed as he leaned into the chair back.

"What do you mean?"

"Look at you. You look horrible. This has only been going on for a few days."

"Are you kidding me, Jarum? This is a colossal fuck up, and beyond that, I have come to you multiple times in the last few weeks about my concerns with our perception in the media. You keep lapsing. Sometimes you wander off mid-conversation. What the hell am I supposed to do with that? Look, I love you, no matter how you treat me, and I always will, but excuse me if I don't look well and can't disassociate from reality as you do."

"What did you just say to me?"

Jarum's tone was a solid bass with no warmth, the drum beat before the war.

Kenny got to his feet.

"Is it the serum? Which one did you take? Every patient taking the direct plasma distillate is beginning to do this. The newer, purer forms are accelerating it."

"What the hell are you talking about?"

Jarum could feel the heat growing within him, his vision narrowing.

"Jarum, this is serious. Let's contain this first problem, but then we need to talk about the hallucinations. It's leaking into the media. We've written it off as a few people with mental illness since people can do it at a med spa at their own risk, but how long will that excuse work? Our earliest patients are showing signs now. We can't get to all of them and cover it up. Doctors are asking questions and threatening to go to the FDA. I need you clear-headed and think you are suffering the same thing."

Something crunched beneath Jarum's fingers as he felt his fist clench. It was like he was outside his body, moving involuntarily, yet he couldn't see. Everything was a blur. He could feel the heat, see the ever-growing yellow illumination seep into his field of vision, and the hum of the wings.

A shiver ran through his body, and Kenny's face materialized above him, red with asphyxiation as his hand clenched tighter on his throat.

"Shit," Jarum said, releasing his grip and stepping back.

Kenny fell into the chair, harsh gasps escaping his lips and clutching his throat.

"Kenny, I..."

A knock sounded at the door.

"Not now!"

Jarum's voice was higher than usual, panicked. He didn't know how he had come to hold Kenny, and while he felt remorse for almost ending a resource he still needed, his concern was that he wasn't conscious of all of his decisions.

"Sir?"

A blonde woman peered in before entering the room entirely. She approached, unaffected by Kenny's wheezing form, and handed Jarum a tablet with streaming footage of Ruth Jarlsen at a gas station in upstate New York.

Jarum met her gaze. Her eyes were almost lifeless as if nobody was home behind the wheel, and her smile seemed painted on, lacking all sincerity.

"Why is she there?"

"Not sure, sir, but we still have the nano-tracker on her that was injected with Ambrosh 31. Her daughter seems to have forgotten the releases she signed when she made her mother's appointment. Her mother's condition level was still considered in the trial phase. She's our property until we release her."

"Find her and bring her back."

The woman's smile expanded slightly but never reached her eyes, her perfect beauty a mask.

"We have reason to believe Am31 was headed in that same general direction, sir."

The room stilled.

"Explain."

"Traffic cameras caught sight of the vehicle they were in just an hour ago on the same highway."

"Send the hunters. I want them all found by any means necessary."

The woman let out a throaty laugh.

"Yes, sir."

Jarum turned away from her, and his gaze fell on Kenny in the chair, his eyes meeting his. He saw only fear and felt the final lifeline to his humanity shatter like a rock through a pane of glass.

He turned away and left Kenny, gasping for life.

CHAPTER NINETEEN

Light drifted in, haloing her in divine likeness. Mama.

"Step away from her," she said, hand outstretched at Ruth, finger pointed in the act of command and judgment.

"Mama!"

She nodded as everyone stared at her, the uncertainty palpable.

"I'm right here, baby. Now come over here and step away from those women."

Kami looked at Violet, who backed away, lowering her eyes in surrender.

Ruth was not as pliable.

"Who are you, and who do you think you are being here?"

Mama met Ruth's gaze. Something unseen shifted in the air, and it became heavier.

"Listen, I think there is some misunderstanding here. My mother knew this place long ago, but maybe it's best if we leave."

Julia's words rang hollow as Mama and Ruth stared at one another, the distant thrum of insectile wings faintly carrying in the space between them.

"Mama?"

Kami looked at Julia as she moved slowly to her mother, hand outstretched with the scissors still directed at Ruth.

Julia tried again.

"Mom!"

Ruth gasped and diverted her gaze, shoulders slumped as something passed between Mama and her. The beating wings stopped.

Kami lurched forward, embracing her mother. She had been praying this moment would come for so long, always sensing she was still out there waiting for her. But why had she left?

Kami's Mama squeezed tighter as though she could sense her daughter's question, willing her to understand from her touch. But Kami withdrew slowly to take her mother in as she did so, not wanting to let her go but needing to face her.

"Mama, why?"

Tears glistened in her mother's eyes, her face soft with sadness.

"They came for me, baby. The men arrived with guns, and somehow I knew they would."

"Your wisdom."

Mama laughed.

"Yes, baby, my wisdom. Though, leaving you unprotected doesn't fit with that. I didn't mean for that to happen. I needed to shake them to come back for you. I'm not sure how long I was on the street, but... Kami, baby, I saw them take Shawn."

Her mother suddenly grew in height; no, the room

shifted vertical dimensions as she fell backward, the floor meeting her to stop any further descent. The wood was smooth and solid, and while she knew she wouldn't plunge any further, her mind still reeled, fleeing from her control.

"I have her," Mama's voice was curt, face tight, as she kneeled, enveloping her and warding off the other women.

"I couldn't help him. I would have if I could, but I couldn't. I was hiding from them not far from the school in an alley, and they... they grabbed him, baby. They were lying in wait."

Mama buried her face into Kami's hair, muffling her words to all those out of earshot. All but Kami.

"I almost thought they were waiting for me and saw the opportunity to grab an unsuspecting black boy as a consolation, but the way they pounced... they targeted him, baby. Too many others had walked past for that not to be true. It's like they knew..."

Kami pulled back to look at her mother, face wilted and eyes downcast.

"Knew about..." Kami couldn't finish.

"Yes, about your connection. Afterward, I came back home for you. I searched, but I could never find you. The dreams, they told me to come here, and I saw you through them. I knew I would hold you again just as those men would come for me.

I've seen things. This thing they're doing isn't natural. There's a reckoning coming."

A hand rested on Mama's shoulder, and they both looked up. The world had ceased to exist, but for them, the other three women forgotten. They encircled them, their approach unnoticed.

Ruth gave Mama's shoulder a squeeze.

"What reckoning?"

Mama and Kami stood and faced Ruth. The veil of Ambrosh31 glistened over her features, but Mama could sense the porcelain-like fragility. Every contour of Ruth's face was enhanced to a photoshop level quality, an overexposure that left glaring signs of the removed blemishes.

This woman wasn't whole.

"Kami and Shawn are both inside you."

"What?" Kami asked, stepping back, feeling Shawn's touch against her cheek and smelling a hint of Old Spice soap. "Shawn?"

Mama appraised Ruth, the downturn of her lip declaring her distaste.

"What that company gave you was made from my baby and her friend. I can sense it in you."

"That isn't possible," Violet said, stepping forward.

"No?" Mama asked, eyebrow arched.

"I don't even know the name of Brosh31. How could you?"

"I can feel it like the darkness this one brings. Kami's boy, his spark, glimmers around her just as surely as my baby's. Your company knew. Something about their connection burns brighter. That man will burn the world."

Mama flicked her wrist at Ruth, her stance fortified like a wall against a storm.

"The dreams... she's the woman of darkness. The fireflies."

Mama nodded.

"The angels more like it. They are the remnants of those changed by this devilry. Every person loses that piece of themself, that glimmer of their soul and memories that flutters away... I can catch them, though. They bring the light, baby. They are trying to blot out the dark."

Ruth sneered.

"How dare you judge me. You don't even know me. The dark? You think I'm some devil?"

"Not entirely of your own making, but time is running short. We three have seen it. We're connected, you see. Not just from the blood you took from my baby but also from what your family did, but we don't have time for that now. You've brought the darkness. They are coming."

CHAPTER TWENTY

T he men spread out in the tall grass, creating a perimeter around the cabin. Several drones flew overhead, controlled by operators back in their vehicles on the main road. They had complete reconnaissance. Nobody would be slipping past them this time.

The forward team approached slowly, determining who was present and what targets needed to be neutralized or acquired. The cabin was more packed than anticipated.

The revelation was radioed almost immediately that all three women were present, a stroke of luck Jarum Daughtry didn't think was possible. But fortune smiled upon him.

"Sir, that's not the only thing. Codename Bethany is here. We have her in our sights."

Jarum leaned forward in his chair, mouth salivating. The girl's mother had been found. The last piece of the puzzle. With her in hand...

"Secure the perimeter, Jon. Once that is done, we must capture Bethany; all the others are trivial. Eliminate them and dispose of the bodies. I am coming there myself."

"Yes, sir."

Jon had his orders, and he would carry them out. For the greater good, he knew he was doing the right thing. He'd been debriefed on Codename Bethany months ago when they first intercepted her. Her DNA matrix had been found to hold the additional markers that could be replicated to fix the one flaw in Lazarus's elixirs, the blackouts.

Most didn't know of them, with the company being so deeply shrouded in secrecy. Still, Kenny Hotchkins called him in occasionally to help keep it under wraps, letting him into the circle and promoting him to lead the security and acquisition teams. He knew what they were fighting for.

The lesser would label them monsters, but history would remember them as heroes.

"Everyone is in position, captain."

Jon nodded.

"Move out."

CHAPTER TWENTY-ONE

The dream took them.

Kami's senses were overwhelmed as a flood of olfactory stimulants, from honey suckles to fresh grass, bombarded her. The buzzing of wings was a crescendo coming from all directions. She spun in place, trying to determine its source as the warm yellow glow crept around her.

"Baby, it's ok," her mother's voice soothed; it was close but muffled as though they were underwater.

Kami followed it, the music of her life, and a radiance, a shining sun, winked into being before her. The void was next to her, a blackhole lashing at her Mama's brilliance like tentacles trying to ensnare its aquatic prey.

The buzzing grew louder, and a swarm of fireflies materialized, flooding the void, filling it. The light shone brighter, and Mama's light blazed like never before.

"She doesn't know what she's brought, child. It's too late. Wake!"

Kami gasped and noticed the same look of distress on Mama and Ruth's faces. They had both been there, too; she hadn't been alone.

"What the hell was happening?" Julia asked, her voice several octaves too high.

"You were glowing, and M-mom, you practically became a shadow."

"I became a shadow?" Ruth's mouth was agape as she turned to Mama.

"I tried to cleanse you, to fill you with light. I don't know how to fix the darkness. Whatever those evil people gave you tainted you, but your purpose will be met. This is how it needed to be; I see that now. You'll atone."

Ruth's eyes were wide, the disbelief plain to everyone.

"What do you mean by my purpose? Atone for what? Just tell me."

Mama sighed, nodding her head. "You need to know, I suppose. This home," Mama lifted her hands, swiveling her arms to encompass the cabin," it wasn't yours. It wasn't your family's until they took it."

"Now, wait a minute. I came here as a child. It was in the family-"

Mama raised her hand, cutting Ruth off.

"We don't have time to debate what you remember. Your mother got the home alright after her affair with my grandfather. Imagine what happened to him once word got out about his relations with a white woman... what she had to say about it once confronted by her family. Times were very different back then, even in the North."

Mama's eyes seethed with hardly contained rage, and all the other women, all those but Kami, hung their heads.

"Yeah, I don't need to explain it all to you. My mother was sent away with him. What was left of him anyway."

Ruth's head snapped up, meeting Mama's eyes. Mama nodded.

"I told you there's a reason we are all drawn to each other. It isn't just Kami's blood flowing through your veins... mine's already there."

Mama's head whipped to the side, head cocked.

"I can feel their whispers right outside. We don't have any time left."

Julia and Ruth stepped forward, their eyes dazed as they tried to take everything in.

"Feel their whispers? My Mom has a sister? What are you talking about, lady?" Julia's voice was near hysterics.

Violet stepped forward with urgency, grabbing Kami's arm.

"We have to go. I didn't get you out of there for someone or something to grab us now. Nothing I see here makes sense."

Kami pulled her arm free from Violet's grasp and brandished the scissors at her.

"No, I won't leave Mama."

"You will."

Mama's voice was hardly audible, yet it seemed to boom to the other women. The air reverberated with her.

She nodded.

"Now you understand when I say I can feel their whispers. There is a whole chorus out there. I will do what I can to distract them. Get Kami out of here.

I've known that I would hold my baby again, but I see

only darkness from this point forward. I've had visions of this meeting ever since they came for me."

Mama looked at Ruth.

"Now you know everything. Hopefully, I've filled you with enough light to blind them from seeing you, but I just don't know. You have to hide Kami and bring light on that man. You know who I mean. The head of the serpent."

Ruth nodded, back straight.

"Jarum Daughtry. That son of a bitch."

Mama gave a nod of approval and moved to the window, each one of her steps equal to two of anyone else's.

Shadows danced in the moonlight, armed men moving swiftly in crouched positions across the clearing to the cabin. They looked like soldiers storming an insurgents bunker.

"Go," Mama whispered, and a crack shattered the silence, punctuating her command.

The glass shattered, mixed with a scream. Mama shifted to the left, falling to the floor. Everyone dropped, following her lead, except for Violet, her body tossed violently backward, glimmers of red spraying into the dusty air.

"Kami!"

"I'm ok, Mama," she said as she army crawled to where Violet was sprawled. A hole about an inch in diameter gushed blood from her side, and color left her face like paint from an overturned can.

Ruth and Julia moved back, huddling into the kitchen as the whispers outside grew to audible shouts; commands to converge on the cabin.

Dust swirled as Mama pivoted to face the older women.

"Get my baby out of here now. Kami, leave her. She's gone."

"She saved me."

"Exactly. Don't let that be in vain. Get to the back door!"

As Julia reached for Kami's arm to pull her away from Violet's still body, Mama stood and faced the blown-out window.

She lifted her arms, and a roar Kami'd only heard in her dreams burst forth as a crescendo of wings split the air. A supernova exploded around them causing everyone to cower on instinct as thousands of fireflies coalesced around Mama, flaring their light in unison.

Gunshots could be heard all around as small pops through the constant buzz. Men yelled, wood cracked, people screamed, glass shattered, and the hum, like the drumbeat of war, roared like thunder.

Ruth pushed the front door open, and Kami and the two women crawled outside, bullets piercing the walls just above their heads. Shadows danced across the gravel driveway as the light Mama unleashed blazed brighter than the sun on the other side of the cabin, thick clusters of fireflies buzzing through the air and field, overwhelming the armed men. They stumbled and flailed, walking within feet of their prone bodies, the insects glowing brightly in their eyes and crawling into their open mouths, burning them out into empty husks of men.

"We have to run to the car now," Julia said, grabbing Kami and Ruth's sleeves as she stood.

The cabin walls began to glow as the light flared through the open doorway and seeped through every crevice in the wood beams. Mama stood in the center, a white-hot silhouette. She waved her arms in slow choreographed arcs, a puppeteer directing tentacles made of thousands of fireflies that smashed into soldiers, flattening, tossing, and pulverizing them.

Drones dropped from the sky as mangled wreckage as Mama's fiery battering rams arced upward before crashing back down to obliterate the helicopter at the edge of the clearing.

"Mama," Kami whispered as the two women pulled her away, their shouts of urgency sounding like distant echoes compared to the roar of the fireflies.

The white core turned, and Kami could feel Mama's words to her; gentle reverberations caressing her like a breeze.

"I love you, baby," etching itself onto her soul like an intangible tattoo, and just as suddenly, the light ceased, and Mama's body flew forward, hardly visible as Kami's eyes tried to adjust to the full dark.

The crunch of Mama's body could be heard hitting something inside the cabin, mixed with the rapidity of an automatic weapon being unloaded. She couldn't think to scream, let alone move, as her body was pulled continually backward by Ruth and Julia toward the car.

Mama was gone this time, there wouldn't be any second chances, there was no doubt. These women were all that was left.

Kami felt numb as she was thrown across the back seat, her consciousness hovering outside her body, surveying the sorrow. All her life, she could rely on her mother's constancy, but that light had been snuffed out, a permanent eclipse.

Gravel banged against the side of the car as the tires peeled backward, the scattering of fireflies intercepting bullets as they sailed toward them, extinguishing their light in a spray of luciferin. The glow would have been wondrous if it hadn't been a harbinger of the real danger.

Time slowed around Kami. The floral scent of the air turned rancid with the smell of gunpowder and death. Ruth and Julia moved in slow motion, mouths open, turning back to face her.

"You're beginning to glow. I can see the glimmers shining through the darkness within you," Kami said to Ruth, her voice coming as if in a dream. A pop sounded, jolting the car before it veered out of control into a ditch and flipped, raining glass all around them.

"Mama," Kami mouthed, willing an answer to come. But all that came in return was darkness.

CHAPTER TWENTY-TWO

The helicopter descended, landing roughly in the large field next to the remnants of the cabin. Bodies littered the area, the men's mouths open and charred as if torched. Jarum passed the destruction, hardly giving them notice.

He knew the consequences of coming after this woman; he dreamed of it all that time ago when he used the blood of a young child for a transfusion on himself, citing a study on the youthfulness it could bring, how the plasma was strengthening that of the weaker recipient. He hadn't felt any revitalization, the cancer he was developing slowly eating away at his lymph nodes, but the visions began, and he studied. There were flashes of hope.

It started as an academic curiosity, and the more blood he could procure, draining it like the proverbial vampire, the stronger the visions became. He dug deeper, moving from one biofirm to the next and, with every company he infiltrated, with each piece of the puzzle he embezzled, the stronger the visions; the more he felt the pull for that woman—the road to Bethany.

The story of Lazarus was imprinted on Jarum Daughtry's mind, always present with each new milestone no matter the cost; with each new sample he ingested and the corresponding test that showed his cancer receding, the greater his ambition became until it consumed him, for he wasn't the only one getting better, thousands of their patients showed the same results.

Time lapsed. His anger swelled. He drank others' fear like a drug and launched Lazarus, bent on unlocking the key to the human genome by any means necessary. They would eradicate disease, and he'd profit for it.

His product was perfect, or so he thought. Mental decay, his Achilles heel, crept into patients eventually. This wasn't the same as Alzheimer's or dementia; flashes of light and sound overwhelming them being the only symptom, leading some to suicide and mania. The attacks were random, surfacing in all age groups with the ramblings of light and the infernal buzzing, all the while, their beauty remained, a characterization of their former selves.

Jarum knew these images, but he could see deeper. Behind them all was Bethany. She held the key. He would drain and deconstruct her DNA until he harvested every last gene from her body. He would have immortality and rebirth. He would be Lazarus of Bethany. The aftermath of his discoveries would alter the course of human history, and Capitalism and American Consumerism were the perfect prism for this pursuit, the ideal accomplice.

As he stood over her body, crumpled and bullet-ridden, he envisioned the coalescing of the last decade of his pursuits. Success was a flavor on his palate that was more decadent than the richest chocolate and the stimulation more arousing than any sexual encounter he could imagine.

"We finally meet," he said, kneeling down, fingering the

hole in her trachea, and scooping out coagulating blood and flesh.

"Hurry up and bring PVC bags. She's well past reaching exsanguination, and we need to salvage all we can. Jon should know this. Where is he?"

A young man in fatigues knelt with a cache of blood bags and affixed a needle to Codename Bethany's arm.

"He was seeing to a few injured men over there, sir."

Jarum nodded and headed outside in the direction indicated, kicking the body of the woman who killed Bennet as if she was little more than refuse in the gutter. The air was thick and humid, smelling of death. Jon was kneeling next to a man, wrapping bandages around his eyes. He heard Jarum approach and stood.

"Sir."

"She's dead."

"Yes, but we didn't have a choice. The things she did, they weren't-"

Jon cut off suddenly as Jarum grabbed him by the neck and lifted him off the ground, his eyes devoid of humanity.

"You nearly cost me everything, and instead of harvesting her, I find you here tending to them? You knew her importance... this cannot be forgiven."

Jon could only manage a grunt as Jarum shoved a knife into his gut, releasing his intestines to spill out of his body. The motions were smooth and casual, not unlike slicing bread for a meal. He tossed him aside.

His blond assistant approached, handing him a towel, her face unfazed by the savage display.

"Such a pity," she said, *tsking* before walking back to the helicopter, the few remaining men from the hunter team backing away.

"Where are the other women?"

"W-we got them, sir," one of the hunters said, barely able to steady his voice. He stepped aside as four other men came out of the trees, half dragging the two women and the girl, Ruth, out front, with eyes only for Jarum.

CHAPTER TWENTY-THREE

Ruth could feel the fire burning within her, tongues of heat licking her insides and creeping up her throat. The pain intensified, on the cusp of excruciating, but she needed to push forward.

Kami's mother had done something to her, which had been all but confirmed by her the moment before their tires had been shot out.

Ruth thought they would all die as the car smashed into the ditch and flipped, throwing glass into her face and cutting her cheeks. Kami and Julia blacked out almost immediately, and Ruth lay there, murmuring their names.

She refused to let the dark retake her though, and she fought the best she could as the men dragged them out of the car, her nails lashing out, clawing at their eyes but to no avail. Even if she had been able to run, she couldn't leave her daughter and that girl behind, not after the sacrifices she had witnessed.

Their march into the clearing was exhausting and painful. A deep ache in her legs, gut, and head turned into a firestorm, pushing her to her limits, but she would carry on. She knew she had more to do here.

It wasn't entirely clear to her that the baton had been passed when she met the woman she knew only as Mama, but in their confrontation, the light that spilled into her was more than a sensation on a dreamlike plane of existence. It had been a transference. Her body was filled to bursting with light, muted by the void Ambrosh31 and her family's sin created inside her. There was something evil tainting that genetic manipulation passed off as a scientific cure, and it altered her. It pushed her prophetic delusions one step further, as if she were the one destined for this showdown.

All she could think about as they were pushed back to the cabin was, why her? She didn't want to be part of this white savior problem. Then she saw him, and they locked eyes. It all made sense; the girl's Mama told her as much.

She wasn't destined to be the hero. Mama chose her to be the Trojan horse. To atone and carry the light as only someone with her blood could. With all the years she had lived, she never thought this would be the turn society would take. Manipulation of the body run amok. Ruth decided no matter how many more years she was granted to live, if Jarum Daughtry's world was the answer, she wanted no part of it.

She embraced the inferno, and it began to boil within. She owed Mama that much. She owed the girl.

"Ruth, Ruth, Ruth. What am I going to do with you?"

Jarum lowered his face to hers and lifted her chin so their faces were level, his pupils mere pinpricks in a pool of blue ice.

"Die," she said, opening her mouth wide. A scream,

soundless but unrestrained in its ferocity, burst forth. Waves of force, visible as they pulsated outward, launched light, brighter even than the flare Mama released, into Jarum's face. The impact erupted with the flash of a supernova, blinding everyone who bore witness and engulfing them both.

CHAPTER TWENTY-FOUR

Violet held Kami's hand, leading her through the dark. She couldn't see, she could hardly feel, the swirling scent of death mixing with that ever-so-familiar honeysuckle, a sickly brew that turned her stomach.

"Witness," Violet kept saying, her voice like a phantom on the breeze, not quite decipherable, but Kami could feel the command tugging at her.

They kept moving through the dark, Violet pulling ever harder, unrelenting. "Stop," she mouthed, but she couldn't get the words out, something holding them back.

"Witness."

They came to a clearing, and the darkness began to glow, a blackish hue as a parody of sunlight.

Ruth was kneeling before Jarum Daughtry, and her core began to pulse, a soft light that grew stronger with every revolution. It was like a firefly. With every infinitesimal movement of Jarum's body, the pulses came faster and flashed brighter.

His finger lifted her chin, and the light hummed loudly with each interval, like a generator under strain, near the point of over capacity.

Jarum's mouth moved, a miasma leaking out, grasping her lips, trying to pry them open to refill her with his poison.

Time stopped, and Kami felt a rush of warmth move through her, a bar of light, white-hot that floated toward Ruth. Kami wanted to scream, to plead, anything for that last chance to say goodbye, but the bar of light moved to Ruth's side and commanded in a voice that sounded like the blaring of trumpets, but Kami knew it was Mama in all her glory, "now."

Ruth opened her mouth, and everything turned white.

Kami woke, her eyes meeting Julia's above her. She was caressing her forehead and looked the worse for wear, but they were alive.

"What happened?"

"I think you would know better than me. You see things that I can't even begin to understand," Julia said.

She looked straight ahead, and Kami sat up. The sun was rising in the East, and the air smelled of grass and dew. There was nothing in front of them but scorched earth.

The flowers, the cabin, the hunters, Jarum, Ruth, Mama... nothing was left, just a blackened circle of dirt, ash, and salt.

Kami looked back to Julia and could see the fatigue on her face, the puffiness that let her know there weren't any more tears to shed.

"They're gone...."
Julia nodded, "Without a trace."

EPILOGUE

*"*In a remarkable turn of events in the absence of the missing CEO Jarum Daughtry, Lazarus COO, Kenny Hotchkins, was sentenced to life in prison for his willing participation in the abduction and confirmed murder of 137 children who were harvested for genetic experimentation that advanced the company's products.*

The most damning evidence leading to this conviction was the testimony of Kami Reynolds, aka Am31, a girl who was abducted and bled but was able to escape with the assistance of a doctor at the facility.

Her first-hand account of what she went through and her corresponding 'rooms filled with bodies' allegations helped lead to the raiding of the company's facilities and, ultimately, to a class action criminal lawsuit before a Grand Jury that put America, and the World, on pause.

With this sentencing concluded, tomorrow begins hearings on Capitol Hill to investigate the flagrant disregard for ethics that seems rife in the biotech industry. Many business leaders fear this could lead to new regulations and lobbyists-"

Kami closed the streaming app on her phone and finished brushing her hair in the mirror. Nothing she said or did could bring any of them back-Mama, Ruth, Violet, or any other children like her that suffered at Jarum Daughtry's hand-but she could at least see that there was finally a bit of justice.

"Kami, dinner," Julia called, her voice echoing up the stairwell.

"Coming."

She smiled at herself in the mirror, trying to see how it felt for Julia's sake. She didn't know how to be happy again after so much pain, but she would try. Mama would want that; after all, they'd found family.

The picture of Mama holding her as a baby, edges tattered, fluttered gently in the breeze from the window. Her heart ached, but underneath it all, she felt that faintest glint of happiness, fortifying the smile she saw herself making in the mirror.

"For you, Mama," Kami said, kissing the picture and taping it back to the mirror. Her life changed direction, but the constants would always be the same in her heart.

I'll never let you go.

Kami brushed her finger across Mama's face a final time and turned off the light in her bathroom, leaving to join Julia and Stacie, the new sister she never dreamed of having, downstairs.

The steady drip from the faucet echoed in the sink, and a single point of light flickered into life in the mirror. It danced and pivoted, illuminating the dark before landing on the picture of Mama- a single firefly pulsing with its golden hue.

It crawled to place itself over Kami in her mother's arms

and spread its wings, fluttering them and causing a faint ripple in the air.

As the little buzz grew louder, it projected its light forward, casting its brilliance over the entire bathroom like a lightbulb, bringing the artificial day to the night.

Mama's love was there, and it shone.

AFTERWORD

The idea for this book first came to me after reading an article by CBS News in February 2019 about a startup company that used young people's blood to treat older patients. The FDA issued a warning that halted these treatments, but all I could think about for days after reading it was, what if?

Like most of my initial ideas, this concept needed time to marinate, and it did so for a solid year as I worked on other story ideas before it burst forth in a flurry of words in March 2020, amidst the opening throes of COVID. It abruptly halted, suspended in a state of stasis, amongst my other pandemic activities (RIP sourdough starter).

This pause raised many questions: Was it a short story or something greater? Should it stay aligned with reality or drift into something otherworldly? Which characters were villains, and who was really the hero of this tale?

Only time would tell as I oscillated between thoughts and inspirations. Every time I revisited my first draft, it morphed into something I initially didn't anticipate. All the while, we as a human race went through an unprecedented global crisis that saw us seeking out experimental options to protect our own lives (whether that be newly minted vaccines or bizarre cure-alls championed by those on the fringe). They were crazy times, and each twist and turn made me take a step back to think.

Ultimately, I am so glad I gave Lazarus the space to sprout into the full story it became and used this time for Kami, Ruth, Julia, and Jarum to take on lives of their own.

Now, this didn't all happen in a bubble. There were people who had to put up with me on this journey, so thank you's are in order.

The biggest thank you goes to my husband Justin, my daughter Graysen, and my Mom (the eternal cheerleader) as I continue to pursue my writing career. They have had to listen to, I don't know how many ideas or dreams of mine as I fleshed out my stories.

Another big thank you to editor Emma Borges-Scott, who helped me structure Lazarus and asked the necessary questions to grow my characters into the beings they'd become.

Lastly, thank you to Caleb Thompson and Kandice Hart, my fellow gods and goddesses of literature podcast mates, who have been with me for most of my writing journey and will always be my first beta readers.

I hope you've enjoyed Lazarus as much as I've enjoyed breathing life into it. Until next time!

BOOKS BY CHRIS KAUZLARICH

ABOUT THE AUTHOR

Chris Kauzlarich is the author of the horror short story collection *Menagerie in the Dark* and the novellas *LAZARUS* and *Moody Road*. A member of the Horror Writers Association, the International Thriller Writers, the Authors Guild, AWP, and the Chicago Writers Association, he writes dark fiction that unsettles precisely because it lives so close to home. A graduate of Purdue University, Chris lives with his husband and daughter between Chicago, IL, and Naples, FL — or somewhere on the open road in their RV, where the best and worst ideas tend to find him.

To stay updated with Chris and discover new books, connect with him on social media or sign up for his newsletter at chriskauzlarich.com.

facebook.com/Writer.Chris.Kauzlarich

instagram.com/chris.kauzlarich

goodreads.com/kauzlarichc1

amazon.com/author/chriskauzlarich

threads.com/@chris.kauzlarich

bookbub.com/authors/chris-kauzlarich

DID YOU LOVE THIS BOOK?
CONSIDER LEAVING A REVIEW

I hope you enjoyed *LAZARUS* by Chris Kauzlarich. If you did, would you leave a review? Nothing helps an author more than readers spreading the word so others can discover it as well.

Please use the QR code or website link below to leave a review on Goodreads. If it isn't too much trouble, could you also leave a review at the place where you purchased it? I will be eternally grateful :)

Thank you again for your support, and happy reading!

https://www.goodreads.com/book/show/198676078-lazarus